SPELLSINGER

AVALON

~ WEB OF MAGIC ~

BOOK 5

SPELLSINGER

RACHEL ROBERTS

Seven Seas

SPELLSINGER

Published by Seven Seas Entertainment.

ISBN: 978-1-933164-72-4

Cover and interior illustrations by Allison Strom

Interior book design by
Pauline Neuwirth, Neuwirth & Associates, Inc.

Printed in Canada
10 9 8 7 6 5 4 3 2 1

You are invited to the
Ravenswood Wildlife Preserve
Benefit Concert

Share the magic of this musical event!

WOODS
OWL CREEK
BIRD SANCTUARY
EAGLE RIDGE
WOODS
OWL CREEK
DEER
MEADOW
BAMBOO
FOREST
HIDDEN FALLS TRAIL
PORTAL
FIELD
MIRROR
LAKE
MAGIC GLADE
SWAN LAKE
TRAIL
ROCKING
STONE
SWAN LAKE
HEDGE
MAZE
TURTLE
BOG
CHITAKAWAY RIVER
TOPIARY
GARDENS
WOLF RUN
PASS
WATER
GARDEN
ROSE
GARDENS
ADRIANE'S
HOUSE
SCULPTURE
GARDENS
RAVENSWOOD
MANOR
MIST TRAIL
MAIN GATE
STONE WALL
PLAYING
FIELDS
MAIN ROAD

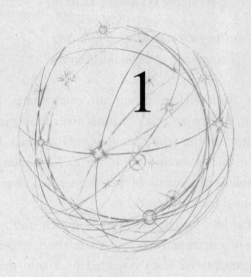

1

I'm in my moon phase, my pink days
When everything is okay
I am beautiful, invincible
Perfectly impossible

The music blasted through Kara's stereo, filling her bedroom with the rockin' sounds of Be*Tween. She slid across the polished wood floor, wildly shaking her head of golden hair. Stomping her pink-socked feet to the beat, she spun into a carefully choreographed move and leaped into her closet.

I'm a free bird, a magic word
The sweetest sound you've ever heard

I've got a sure thing, a gold ring
I'm waking up my wildest dreams

Clothes went flying, piling up everywhere. Kara hopped out, pulling on a pair of jeans and slipping into a blue sweater at the same time. Lyra's spotted head popped out from a mound of clothes as Kara spun past the bed, pulling the cat up by her front paws, sweeping the big animal back and forth.

Kara bent low, feeling the rhythm launch into a jangling wave of guitars and synths. Lyra fell back into a pile of stuffed animals as Kara bounded high into the air, flinging her arms wide. Spinning around, she grabbed her hair dryer and sang into it:

And nothing in this world can change it
Turn me round or rearrange me
Love is all that matters lately 'cause
I'm on a supernatural high

Kara's voice rang out, loud, happy—and completely off key. But that didn't matter. Lyra lay on her back in the middle of Kara's stuffed audience tapping her paws. Kara dove into the fluffy mountain and tickled the cat's belly, causing Lyra to yelp as they both sang along with their favorite new band.

Kara was multitasking: dressing, dancing, singing, and celebrating all at the same time. She was so cool—life

was so cool. Since she had received word that Be*Tween would play at the Ravenswood Wildlife Preserve benefit concert, Kara had been pumped, playing their new songs nonstop. No one believed she could really pull this off,. but she had stayed focused and determined, stationing herself at Town Hall every day for the past two weeks. A barrage of e-mails and a phone call from her dad, Mayor Davies, had convinced Be*Tween's manager that the popular girl band could make a stop in Stonehill.

She danced over to her desk, stuffed a stack of papers into her new briefcase, and snapped it closed. When she put her mind to something, there wasn't anything she couldn't do. And for the first time since Kara had convinced her dad to let her, Adriane, and Emily become tour guides for the preserve, the council actually seemed excited. All except Beasley Windor, who had made it her personal task to keep an eye on the girls. Mrs. Windor had wanted the old Ravenswood Manor torn down and the land redeveloped into a country club and golf course. But thanks to Kara, this was going to be the event of the year and it would be Ravenswood—1, Windor—0.

Outside, a horn honked. Kara turned to Lyra. "It's show time!"

"Already?" Lyra peeked out from the behind the bed where she had toppled onto a comfortable pillow.

Kara heard the cat's voice in her mind. At first it had felt odd, but now it was like second nature, as if she and the magical cat had been best friends forever.

She opened the big window over her desk. "I'll see you at Ravenswood."

Lyra leaped to the windowsill, brushing her face against Kara's. "*Later.*"

"Love you." Kara gave the cat a quick kiss and ran for the door.

She took the stairs two at a time. "Mom! I'm going! Dad's taking me over to Ravenswood!"

"Okay," Mrs. Davies called from her study. She sounded preoccupied; she was probably working on another divorce case or something.

"I have a big meeting with the council about the benefit!" Kara yelled. For a second she wished her mom would show just a little interest in all of her hard work at Ravenswood. Well, this concert would be hard to ignore! Cheered by that thought, she shot out the front door, bolting into a crisp October morning.

"*Are you okay?*" Lyra peeked out from behind a hedge.

"Of course. Go before my dad sees you," Kara called out as the big cat slunk into the woods bordering the Davies' property. A golden glow ran up and down the cat's spotted back as two large wings unfolded.

"And don't let anyone see you flying!"

"*Cats don't fly.*" In a moment, Lyra was soaring over the Chitakaway River and into the dense woodlands beyond.

Kara ran across the front lawn to the dark green Lexus waiting in the driveway. She hopped into the passenger seat, popping down the sun visor to check her hair in the mirror. "Hi, Daddy."

"All ready, princess?" the handsome mayor of Stonehill smiled, running fingers through his graying but thick hair.

"I have all the papers right here." She smiled, showing off her new leather case, a gift from the Mayor's staff. They'd been very impressed with the diligence of Ravenswood's young president. At least *some* people appreciated her efforts.

"You still have to get final approval from Mrs. Windor and the rest of the Ravenswood committee for the construction of your stage," Mayor Davies reminded her, pulling the car out of the driveway.

"No prob, Mayor Davies. Everything's under control."

BEASLEY WINDOR TAPPED her foot impatiently, beady eyes darting back and forth. She raised the large lion's head door knocker and pounded away at the front door to Ravenswood Manor. A few members of the council were with her, including Sid Stewart, Lionel Hoover, and Mary Rollins.

"We haven't seen anything unusual so far, Beasley," Lionel remarked.

"Just keep your eyes open," Mrs. Windor said, scanning the trails leading into thick woods. "Something strange is going on out here, and I'm going to find out what."

"Hoo doo yoo doo."

Startled, Mrs. Windor spun around. Emily walked across the gravel driveway toward the group. A great snowy owl was perched on the girl's shoulder. The owl's flared wing tips sparkled with flecks of turquoise and lavender. Mrs. Windor eyed the owl suspiciously. She could have sworn the owl just spoke. No one else seemed to have heard anything unusual. But the girl, Emily . . . did she just give that bird a warning look?

"Hi, everyone," Emily said, quickly stroking the owl's wings closed. "Er . . . Kara's on her way and Adriane must be in the library at the computer."

"Hello, Emily. We hear your Ravenswood Web site has gotten quite a few hits," Sid Stewart said.

Emily smiled. "It's getting really busy! We've been posting information on animals, ecology, and environmental issues. We all have to think 'green' you know."

"Very interesting," Mary Rollins said, clearly impressed.

"Yes, and our teacher is giving us extra credit for sharing it with the school." Emily looked at Mrs. Windor. "I'd be happy to show you—"

"I want to see everything!" Mrs. Windor snapped. "And I want a list of every animal here on the preserve. Every since that *peculiar* incident at Miller's Industrial Park, animals have shown up at the mall and even at the school. Your disruption at the football game with that—*horse* thing was too much!"

Emily winced, thinking about the unicorn, Lorelei. Emily had felt such a strong bond with her. Although the unicorn had been gone for only a few weeks, Emily missed her greatly. "We thought the Stonehill Sparks could use a mascot. It would tie into the whole theme of Ravenswood Preserve being such an important place for animals."

"You're saying a *unicorn* represents the theme of Ravenswood?" Mrs. Windor snickered.

"No . . . it's just . . ."

"Oh c'mon, Beasley," Sid chuckled. "It was just a make-believe unicorn. Very imaginative, too."

"And the kids loved it," added Lionel. "Our team won."

Mrs. Windor glared at Emily. "Just what kind of animals are you hiding here?" she asked accusingly.

From the corner of her eye, Emily saw Lyra drop from the skies behind the manor.

"Just the ones that live here . . . I mean—" she sputtered nervously.

"We do have a deal with the Town Council, if you remember, to protect *all* the animals that live here," said a new voice.

Everyone turned as Nakoda, Adriane's grandmother and the official caretaker of Ravenswood, emerged from the front door of the manor. "In the absence of the owner, Mr. Gardener, the girls have done a wonderful job managing Ravenswood."

"Our *deal* is to see if the preserve makes economic sense for the town," Mrs. Windor countered.

"And we're willing to open the preserve for a benefit concert," Gran reminded her. "With a percentage of the profits going to the Stonehill Council."

"Assuming there *are* profits," Mrs. Windor said. "You're asking us to pay for some rock and roll concert when this land could be used to benefit everyone."

"Tourism dollars are the backbone of many small communities," Lionel mused.

"Not to mention the press this should generate," Sid added.

"You'll see," Emily said. "It's going to be great."

"It's not going to *be* anything at all, young lady," Mrs. Windor reminded her. "Not until *we* say it is."

The mayor's Lexus pulled into the wide circular driveway and came to a stop. Kara bounded out. "Hey, kids!"

"Ah, Mayor Davies," Lionel said as he walked to the mayor to shake his hand. Sid was right behind him.

"Greetings, Sid, Lionel, Mary. A beautiful day, isn't it, Beasley?"

"Mayor Davies," Mrs. Windor said gruffly, wagging her finger. "I expect a complete breakdown of this proposed event."

"Right! I have all the specs right here." Kara flipped her hair back and opened her briefcase.

"Good day to you, Nakoda." The mayor bowed to Gran and turned to face Mrs. Windor. "Kara has it all worked up, Beasley," he said.

Kara smiled and glanced down at the papers and gasped. They were all out of order!

Emily slid in with a save. "Come on, we'll show you where the event will take place out on the great lawn."

Shuffling papers, Kara followed Emily as she herded the group along the path that led to the back lawn bordered by resplendent gardens. The surrounding trees were ablaze with the colors of autumn.

A sudden rustling made Mrs. Windor look around furtively. Something with soft blue and pink fur danced past the trees.

"The stage will go there," Kara pointed out quickly, managing to draw Mrs. Windor's attention away from the magical animals that should have been safely hidden. That's supposed to be Adriane's responsibility, Kara thought, annoyed.

"The stage is really just a raised platform," Mayor Davies added. "The show goes on from four till six, Saturday afternoon."

Kara finished sorting out the papers and presented them to Mrs. Windor. "It's all right here."

Mrs. Windor glared at Kara as she took the papers.

"With the newest, hottest band coming, to make sure it's a hit!" Kara exclaimed.

"Not exactly."

The group whirled around. Adriane walked toward them, a paper fluttering in her hand. "Be*Tween isn't coming."

"*What?*" Kara ran over to her.

"Look for yourself." Adriane held up a printout.

Kara snatched the e-mail.

Dear Miss Davies,

Unfortunately, Be*Tween will not be able to make an appearance at your benefit concert. The entire tour has been canceled due to unforeseen events. We apologize for any inconvenience.

Joseph Blackpool, CEO
Worldwide Tours Unlimited

"Be*Tween isn't coming." Kara repeated glumly, all the energy draining out of her.

"Well, there goes your little show," Mrs. Windor said with a smirk.

"No way!" Kara said, trying to think fast. "They *have* to show up!"

"They're missing," Adriane said.

"Huh?"

"Word online says Be*Tween vanished. Just disappeared."

"Disappeared? How does a group like Be*Tween just

disappear?" It was probably all part of some bogus publicity stunt to get people talking. And who cares about some little benefit concert, right? Kara kicked a small stone. "That's just great!"

"However . . ." Adriane said with a sly edge to her voice.

"What?" Kara was almost afraid to ask.

"There's a second e-mail." Adriane's dark eyes twinkled as she held up a second printout.

"What? What!" Kara reached for it.

"Let's see here . . ." Adriane teased her, moving the paper out of Kara's clasping fingers.

"Hurry Up! Oh, give me that!" Kara grabbed the e-mail.

Miss Davies,

Further to our last e-mail, we received notice that one of our premier musical performers has volunteered to replace Be*Tween at your benefit event: Johnny Conrad.

Kara's eyes went wide.

"Johnny Conrad . . ." Kara wobbled and sank to the ground. "Johnny Conrad . . . coming here!" she screamed.

"Johnny Conrad? Even I've heard of him!" Mary Rollins exclaimed.

"Wow! He's one of the biggest stars in the world!" Emily said, amazed.

Kara jumped to her feet. "Johnny Conrad is coming here!" She swooned and promptly sat down again.

"Can you believe it?" Adriane grinned. "This town is going to rock!"

"*Ahhh!*" Kara screamed, leaping in the air.

The three girls were hugging and jumping up and down together.

"Well, I would say this event will certainly generate some publicity for Ravenswood," Mayor Davies smiled. "Good work, girls."

"Johnny Conrad!" Kara squealed, stomping her pink sneakers into the grass.

Sid pulled Mrs. Windor aside. "Do you know what kind of crowd a star like this will attract?" he whispered. "Thousands of people are going to show up!"

"Yes . . ." Mrs. Windor smiled evilly. "Think of it, thousands of kids, press, and tourists all coming here to the Ravenswood Preserve."

"This will surely put Ravenswood on the map," Sid said proudly.

"If there's anything left of it after it's over," Mrs. Windor whispered, grinning.

2

kstar: got some news today—Be*Tween can't come and play

chinadoll: :-! what happened?

swandiver: <oo> what's wrong?

goodgollymolly: I just heard their latest song

beachbunny: they didn't break up, did they?

chinadoll: tell me that's not what u'r gonna say ☹'

Sunlight poured through the large round windows of Ravenswood Manor's library, gently caressing Kara's face as she watched the IMs flying across her laptop screen. Drawing a deep breath, she let her fingers dance over the keyboard.

kstar: fear nottest, we got the hottest
goodgollymolly: who could be so cool?
beachbunny: we must tell everyone at school
kstar: Johnny Conrad!
swandiver: Johnny Conrad? I'm scREAMin! :-O O-:
mistyrose: that's incredible!
chinadoll: he's so hot!
beachbunny: Johnny Conrad? i must be dreamin!

A sudden tap on the shoulder made Kara jump half out of her skin. "Hey, Hannah Montana!"

"What?" Kara snapped. She whirled around to see Adriane standing behind her with a grave expression.

"We got a problem," Adriane said. "It's Mrs. Windor. She came in with the construction teams."

"So? Let her boss them around for a bit. Give her something to do."

"She snuck off into the woods. She's out there right now and she's got a camera."

Kara's stomach tightened. "Did you get the feeling that she caved too easily on this concert?"

"Yeah, it had crossed my mind," Adriane said.

"Let's go!" Kara exclaimed.

Logging off, Kara raced with Adriane from the library, down the rear stairs, and out the back of the manor house. About ten men were hauling huge planks of wood across the great lawn. Another group rolled cable and equipment. Others stood looking at a set of plans.

"Where is she now?" Kara asked Adriane.

"Storm, what's happening?" Adriane called into empty air. Instantly, she heard the silver mistwolf's answer in her mind.

"She's headed for the Rocking Stone."

Kara heard, too. "Oh, great! What if she finds the secret glade?" Kara picked up her pace. "What's Storm going to do? Wrestle Mrs. W. to the ground and take her camera?"

"That's why you're here," Adriane grinned. "We need some presidential action."

They flew past the hedge maze and took a path into the woods. Only a small barrier of trees separated the Rocking Stone from the glade where so many of the homeless animals from the magical world of Aldenmor now lived.

Mrs. Windor was determined to shut down Ravenswood through any means necessary; if she could show the Town Council pictures of strange creatures—or even what looked like bizarre animals—running loose in the preserve, she'd almost certainly get her way. And that would only be the beginning. A video would be a sure hit on YouTube and then the truth would be discovered. Scientists or some government agency would take the magical animals away; they would remain in cages, possibly the subject of experiments—or worse—for the rest of their lives.

They could not let that happen to their new friends. Kara and Adriane raced toward the stone marker.

∽◊∽

Beasley Windor tripped half a dozen times on roots she could have sworn were trying to snag her. She had whacked her head twice on low lying branches that she was certain swept in out of nowhere—it simply couldn't have been that she was looking one way and walking another. This was a dangerous place.

It had to go.

Giggling whispers floated through the woods.

Who was that?

A flutter of leaves made Mrs. Windor turn to a large outcropping of willow trees. She carefully tiptoed off the trail.

Hunching over, she peered into the small screen of the digital camera she had borrowed from her niece.

Strange creatures were here, and they were playing games with her. They were certain they had nothing to fear—and that would be their undoing.

"I've got you now," she whispered.

Kara and Adriane hid behind a tree, watching as Mrs. Windor walked directly toward a space between two bushy willow trees.

"She's moving away from the glade," Kara whispered. She couldn't believe their luck—

Adriane gasped, pointing. "Right into trouble."

A pack of duck-like quiffles were pulling a large

branch back tight, ready to let it fly at their unsuspecting visitor. Their big, webbed feet tapped with anticipation as the woman moved closer.

"We've got to do something!" Adriane said urgently.

"We can tell her they're migrating visitors from Canada," Kara suggested.

"Uh-huh, and what about that?" Adriane pointed behind the quiffles. "A visitor from Atlantis?"

Kara's eyes widened. Standing a dozen feet beyond the quiffles, in a pool of warm, golden-glowing light, stood a pony with green and purple wings—a pegasus. All Mrs. Windor had to do was turn to the right with her camera and she would get the video of the year!

"Do something!" Adriane pushed Kara.

"All right, all right. Here." Kara tapped Adriane's jewel.

A searing bolt of golden light ripped from the stone, smashing into a treetop with a terrible explosion.

Whammm-crrrackkkk!

Three quiffles went flying as their branch shot forward. Mrs. Windor shrieked and whirled around—where a collection of seared branches toppled down, quickly piling up to obscure her view of the pegasus.

Adriane gave Kara a stern look. "I didn't say to knock down the whole forest!"

A small blur of gold and brown dashed behind the new barrier, kicking the magical animals away and herding them deeper into the wilds of Ravenswood. Kara breathed a sigh of relief as she saw Ozzie, the magical ferret, give her a thumbs-up—well, actually a paws-up.

Mrs. Windor was frantically looking in every direction. "Who's out there?"

Kara and Adriane poked their heads out from either side of the tree just in time to see Mrs. Windor about to trip over Rommel the wommel!

"Hey, watch where you're—!" Rommel started, but his warning came too late.

Mrs. Windor, still holding onto the camera with trembling fingers, looked into the face of the small, talking koala-like bear. She leaped back, cried out, and tripped, landing in a puddle of mud.

By the time she raised her camera and wiped the lens clean, Rommel had rushed off.

"Come back here you little freak!" Mrs. Windor shouted, spitting out muddy goop.

"Oh no," Kara groaned. What were they supposed to do now?

A sudden gust of wind blew around the woman, a spiral of force that kicked up dirt, twigs, and stone, quickly forming into what looked like a mini-twister!

"Adriane!" Kara hissed. "Stop it!"

The dark-haired girl looked at her wolf stone. The jewel was pulsing with strong amber light. "I'm not doing that!"

Then the ground beneath Mrs. Windor trembled. The whirlwind spun closer to the struggling woman. Mouth agape, she managed to keep the camera focused.

Suddenly, Mrs. Windor's camera was ripped from her hands by a blast of wind. It flew into the air, smashing to pieces against a large stone.

The whirlwind picked up grass, vine, twigs, and leaves, magically forming into a figure made from the earth itself. Sparkling quartz eyes regarded its surroundings.

"It's a Fairimental!" Adriane gasped. "I met one on Aldenmor at the Fairy Glen."

Fairimentals were extremely magical beings, the keepers and protectors of good magic on Aldenmor.

"What's it doing here?" Kara asked.

"Magesss," the twiggy figure rustled, bits of leaves and dirt flying as it wobbled about.

"What the—?" Mrs. Windor looked closer at the creature.

With a sudden shudder, the Fairimental exploded, sending debris everywhere.

Mrs. Windor whirled around and raced back through the woods, howling.

Adriane and Kara ran to the various pieces of the Fairimental. Two tiny whirlpools of dirt and leaves spun from the ground, desperately trying to regain shape.

"Warrior . . ." one said. Rattling crazily, the whirlpool flew apart.

" . . . blazing star . . . terrible danger," the other small pile managed to say. It, too, was starting to break up.

"What's happened?" Adriane asked urgently.

" . . . usse fairy map . . ."

Kara swallowed hard, thinking about the glowing map she had lost.

"Spellsing as three . . ." The Fairimental caved in on itself, shaking violently into a whirling mess. "Before isss too late . . ."

Then whatever force was holding the Fairimentals together abruptly vanished and their elements crumbled to the ground.

Adriane looked at Kara.

The girls knew that the Dark Sorceress of Aldenmor would stop at nothing to find magic, and Avalon was the source of *all* magic. Her most recent attempts to locate Avalon had damaged the magic web itself, the strands of magical energy that connected worlds everywhere, and supposedly, reached all the way to Avalon. As far as the girls knew, the portals to the Fairy Glen on Aldenmor—where the Fairimentals lived—were still missing. No one had seen or heard from the Fairimentals since those portals had disappeared . . . until now.

"What was it trying to tell us about the fairy map?" Adriane asked.

"We already know the sorceress has it." Kara remembered the gift the fairy creature called Phelonius had tried to give her. At the time, she didn't know how important it was. In fact, she didn't know what it was at all. Until it had been stolen and taken back to the sorceress. It was their one clue to finding Avalon.

"Maybe she's trying to use it," Adriane guessed.

"This is just great!" Kara tossed her hands in the air and spun back to face Adriane. "We've got Mrs. Windor about to announce Stonehill's first alien sighting and Johnny Conrad is arriving in two days! We can't have Fairimentals and who knows what else popping up!"

"Maybe we should just postpone the benefit," Adriane suggested quietly.

"No *way!*" Kara stated. "This show is going on! The Fairy Glen and Avalon are just going to have to wait."

Adriane bit her lip as she watched Kara stomp away, heading back to prepare Stonehill for the event of the year.

3

$\mathcal{E}$MILY RACED UP the steps of Stonehill's Town Hall. It was a little after four on Thursday, and hundreds of people were gathered on the sidewalk facing the old red brick building. Main Street had been cleared of parked cars and blocked off, and the park across the street from Town Hall was filled with even more spectators. Photographers and professional TV news crews had descended upon the normally quiet town square.

At the top of the steps, near the front entrance, stood a small podium with a microphone stand. A WELCOME JOHNNY CONRAD banner fluttered above the doors.

A pudgy security guard with curly red hair and freckles stood beside the main doors. "Hello, Emily. Got quite a crowd today."

"Hey, George!" Emily said breathlessly as she slipped past him. She flew down the dark wood-paneled corridor, passing dozens of photographs detailing Stonehill's history. She whipped past an open door where she smelled food and heard laughter. Inside, Mayor Davies and the Town Council gathered in the small room, chatting.

The real activity was centered in the main meeting room. Emily burst through the doors and was nearly run over by Kara's brother, Kyle, and his friend Marcus, who were rushing by with stacks of folding chairs in their arms. The meeting room had been transformed into a reception hall, complete with streamers strung across the walls, balloons bouncing above decorated tables, and a budget-busting buffet piled with enough food to satisfy the entire population of Stonehill—twice!

"Over to the left . . . a bit higher," Kara commanded, standing in the midst of her "troops," more than two dozen volunteers from school. Her buds Heather, Tiffany, and Molly were doing their best to center a big poster of Johnny Conrad on the rear wall.

"It looks great, Kara!" Heather yelled.

"My arm is getting sore," Molly muttered.

"No pain, no party!" Kara hollered. She looked down and brushed the front of her new powder blue sweater, one eyebrow raised defensively at the possibility of a stray crumb.

Resisting the urge to duck and cover, Emily announced herself. "Sorry I'm late, Kara, the McHenrys dropped off their monkeys at the Pet Palace. The monkeys used to be in a circus. You should see them, they're so smart and—"

"Emily!" Kara snapped, cutting her off. "Ice!" She slipped a large bowl into Emily's hands.

"Nice to see you, too," Emily groused, glancing over at Kara's clique. Molly shrugged and waved. Heather held up a small sign with an arrow and pointed it at Kara. It said: GIRL OUT OF CONTROL.

Emily giggled as she headed past them. It felt good to be on the same side as Kara's other friends for once. Maybe this event was exactly what the town needed to come together and support Ravenswood. And it was all thanks to Kara.

"Attention! Johnny will be here at seventeen hundred hours sharp!" Kara bellowed. "That's less than an hour from right now for those of you who haven't been paying attention. Everything has to be perfect!"

Kara's blond hair whipped wildly as she spied her brother and his friend daring to rest for half a second. "Those chairs won't move themselves, you slackers!"

"Aye, aye, *mon capitan*," Marcus snapped to attention, giving Kara a salute.

Smiling, Emily walked into the kitchen. She was just starting to fill the ice bowl when Kara breezed in.

"Everything under control at Ravenswood?"

"Ozzie's in command," Emily answered quietly. "He's under strict orders to keep the animals at the glade."

"He better not let anyone past his fuzzy face," Kara whispered, frowning. "We're lucky Mrs. Windor hasn't said anything about what she saw. Yet."

"Doesn't make me feel any better about what happened."

"We can't worry about that right now." Kara scanned the kitchen for any other slackers.

"It's our job to worry about it." Emily dumped more ice.

"Hey!" Kara yelled at Joey. "Easy on the food, save some for the rest of us!"

"Anyway, we have to stay calm, Kara—Kara?"

"Tick tock," Kara pointed to her watch as she breezed back out of the kitchen.

At ten minutes to the hour, the room was ready. Kara scooted, shooed, and skedaddled the volunteers out of the room and locked it behind her so that *nothing* could be touched. She stood guard alone, eyes darting, another frown forming.

Emily approached cautiously. "Hi. My name is Emily. Can Kara come out to play?"

Kara slumped against the door. "There's just so much going on . . ."

"You're doing a great job," Emily reassured her. "And so is everyone else. It would be nice if they heard that now and then."

"Okay. What do you think we should do about the Fairimental's message?"

"We should contact Zach after the press conference,

when everything calms down," Emily answered, referring to the human boy Adriane had met on Aldenmor.

"Fine. I'll call the d-flies. They can make a portal phone call."

Something *squawked* in Kara's bag. She hauled out a small walkie-talkie.

"Ground control," she said.

"Drone One to Queen Bee," a voice hissed.

"Go ahead, Drone One."

"Target spotted. Headed right toward Main Street. You are not going to believe it!"

"Stay calm, Drone One . . ." Kara urged.

"It's Johnny *Conrad! Ahhhhh!*" The walkie-talkie crackled and cut off.

"We've lost Drone One," Kara said. She quickly checked her watch. "T-minus five and counting. How do I look?" She fluffed her blond hair.

"Perfect."

Kara grinned. "Let's move out!"

They ran into the room where Mayor Davies and the other council members were still chatting away.

"People! People!" Kara hollered. "Let's go. Our guest of honor has arrived!"

"Ooo, how exciting," Mary Rollins exclaimed.

"Let's keep this orderly now," Mayor Davies stated. "Just another visitor to our humble town."

"Look! It's Johnny Conrad!" Heather was jumping up and down, pointing out the front window.

"*Ahhhh!*" Tiffany screamed.

Everyone in the room rushed for the door at once, stampeding past the mayor. Soon the vast crowd outside started screaming.

This was it. Kara was about to become a star.

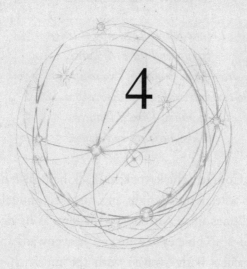

4

OUTSIDE TOWN HALL, Kara stood beside her dad. She heard the rumble of engines and the blare of car horns.

And in the distance . . . music?

Kara's eyes widened as she and everyone else in the enormous crowd turned toward the street, where a jet-black convertible T-bird with the top down drifted their way. A young, dark-haired guy stood on the hood, a microphone in his hand. A tour bus crept along at a respectful distance behind the singer. A guy with sunglasses sat with a mixer board in the back between two huge speakers while another one drove, their heads bobbing to the beat of the thundering, pulsating, blisteringly happening song that was currently topping the charts.

Let me tell you, if I sing it true,
get up and start the dance,
No matter what you do, it's your life, you're you,
So come on and take a chance and dance!
Dance! Dance! Dance!
Take a chance and dance!

Johnny Conrad's thick, tousled black hair glistened in the golden afternoon sunlight and his deep, model-perfect cheekbones filled with dusky shadows as he rapped. His soulful deep blue eyes were cast heavenward and his lanky, muscular body swayed with the music, his pale shirt clinging, his black leather boots and pants shining, his long leather jacket curled behind him. The booming music seemed to ensnare his listeners as everyone moved to the beat. Molly, Heather, and Tiffany were bopping like crazy, dancing around the black car as it rolled up to the curb.

Just take a chance and dance!
Dance! Dance! Dance!
Take a chance and dance!

The entire crowd was caught in the rhythm, the enveloping sound, and the enchantment that was Johnny Conrad. Dancing, moving, shaking, and screaming, adults, teens, and children all rocked out to the sounds of the latest music sensation.

Johnny leaped from the hood, his wireless microphone catching every note as he sang his heart out. Security held the crowds back as Johnny climbed the wide steps of Town Hall, heading right for the podium. The song ended and Johnny took a bow, creating another round of searing screams from his audience. Smiling, he waved and tossed the microphone to his driver.

Mayor Davies stared in slack-jawed wonder at Johnny, who patiently nodded and waved to his fans and the press. Cameras flashed bright lights into the singer's brilliant blue eyes.

"Hello, Stonehill!" Johnny called out.

The crowd erupted in frantic, ear-piercing screams. "Johnny! Johnny!"

Kara was practically beside herself as the superstar approached, but she had a job to do. She nudged her dad's arm, snapping him to attention. She noticed Adriane standing next to Emily, cheering.

Mayor Davies cleared his throat four times, right into the podium's microphone, but nothing happened until Johnny put a single finger to his lips and winked at the adoring crowd—which suddenly fell completely silent.

"They're all yours," Johnny whispered, nodding to the mayor.

Kara watched Johnny, transfixed.

Whoa. This guy was *hot*.

"Johnny Conrad, thank you for taking time out of your mad busy schedule to help the Ravenswood Wildlife

Preserve—your act of super cool generosity has moved us all," Mayor Davies read from the script Kara had written. "The town council would like to offer you and your crew—our best suites at the Stonehill Inn . . . ?" he turned to Kara.

She smiled ear to ear.

The mayor shrugged and continued. "And as mayor of Stonehill, I'd like to present you with the key to our city!"

Covering the microphone, Mayor Davies nodded toward Kara, "I think you've already won the key to my daughter's heart."

"Dad!" Kara wailed.

Johnny smiled at Kara—and she managed not to faint. Then he turned to the crowd and shot them a dazzling smile, holding the big golden key high over his head.

"Thank you very much. We're proud to play for all you fine people. And for the wonderful cause of the Ravenswood Wildlife Preserve." He winked at Kara.

Kara practically leaped into the air.

"And we've got something special planned," Johnny announced. "As part of a promotion for my new CD, *Under Your Spell*—"

Screams erupted, but quieted down as Johnny raised his arms.

"I'm inviting one fan to sing onstage with me during the concert Saturday. The performance will be streaming live all over the world!"

"*Ahhh!*" Kara screamed.

"*Ahhhh!*" dozens of girls screamed with her.

"*Ahhhhhhh!*" the crowd screamed and screamed and screamed some more.

Sid Stewart put his hands over his ears, screaming in pain.

"That's right, we're holding a contest for one special person to sing with me . . ." Johnny eyed Adriane. "To take a chance and dance," he crooned lightly.

From the corner of her eye Kara caught a twinkle at the dark haired girl's wrist. "If I can only find him . . . or her." And then, suddenly, he zoomed in on Kara and seemed to see . . . something. "Maybe I already have."

Kara's heart skipped a beat.

He means me, she thought. *Yes!* He's talking about me!

Kara struggled to control herself. She took a step toward the microphone and was about to speak when Adriane suddenly grabbed the mike.

"Johnny," Adriane said, gazing at the handsome star. "As a representative of the Ravenswood Wildlife Preserve, I want to thank you again for your support of animals all over the world—"

Kara pulled the mike out of Adriane's hands.

"As *president* of the Ravenswood Preservation Society, I want to personally thank you for supporting worldwide wildlife—"

Adriane stepped on Kara's foot and grabbed the mike back. "I'd like to invite you and your crew to stay at Ravenswood Manor," she quickly said, holding the mike away from Kara's grabbing fingers. "What better way to get exposure for Ravenswood than for Johnny Conrad himself to stay there?" She smiled.

"Whoa, Ravenswood Manor." Johnny beamed. "*Now* you're talking!"

No *way!* Emily mouthed to the girls, dumbfounded.

"Outstanding!" Johnny said. "I'd be honored to make Ravenswood Manor my home away from home." He turned to his entourage. "How do you like that for hospitality?"

The members of Johnny's band all nodded enthusiastically. The crowd cheered.

Adriane glanced past Kara at the pop star, her wolf stone glowing. "I can't wait to practice with Johnny."

Kara felt unsteady. What did Adriane think she was doing? Suddenly a flare of magic sparkled in her eyes—then she saw the photographers snapping away.

Kara felt a white-hot fire of fury rise within her. It was all she could do to keep from screaming at the girl. This contest was the most important thing in the world! "I'm going to win that contest," Kara hissed. "It'll be *me* onstage singing with Johnny."

"I guess we'll see about that." Adriane strutted off.

Kara put her best smile on display for the crowd as she and her dad prepared to take the activities inside. The Town Council and their friends and families couldn't wait to meet and greet the great Johnny Conrad.

Ooooh! That Adriane! Finally the real warrior has

surfaced, Kara thought. The one who just *has* to compete with me. Fine, let her try. I will win, Kara thought. *I will!*

There was just one slight glitch: Kara couldn't sing a note in tune if her life depended on it. And everyone knew it.

5

S TREAKS OF LAVENDER stretched across the horizon as stars winked into existence over the forest. Kara and Emily walked down the gravel driveway to Ravenswood Manor. The girls had about an hour before Johnny and his entourage were due to arrive.

"What got into you two?" Emily demanded. "That was the most immature display I've ever seen!"

"I just got so mad! How could she *do* that?" Kara was steaming at Adriane's totally irritating behavior. "She's trying to outdo me, steal my thunder."

"You're not in this alone, Kara," Emily reminded her.

"Then how are *we* going to get the entire Ravenswood Manor ready?"

"I don't know," Emily answered. "We'll just have to keep everyone out of the library."

She stopped at the front doors of the manor. "And we have to keep the magical animals out of sight!"

"About time!" Ozzie called out.

A gathering of animals milled around the cobblestone path to Adriane's house led by Ozzie, Lyra, the pegasus called Balthazar, and Ronif, leader of the duck-like quiffles—all key members of the girls' inner circle of trusted magical animal friends.

"What kept you?" Ozzie asked, crossing his furry ferret arms and tapping a rear paw. "Everyone's waiting for Fairimental updates."

"All we know so far," Emily explained, "is a few came to warn us about possible danger, so I want all of you on high alert."

"I've got Stormbringer and a pack of pooxim on patrol," Ozzie said. "Look out, evil!"

"Adriane returned a short time ago, acting very strangely," Lyra said softly.

"Strange like how?" Kara asked.

"There have been bursts of her magic all through the manor."

Kara and Emily exchanged worried glances.

"Looks like we're going to have some guests for a few days," Emily announced to the animals.

"Who?" Balthazar asked.

"Johnny Conrad!" Kara dramatically swooned.

The animals looked at each other, bewildered. Ronif shrugged.

"I want Lyra, Balthazar, and Ronif with Storm on perimeter watch. Gather the rest back at the glade, Ozzie," Emily ordered. "I need a complete head count."

Ozzie led the animals toward a forest trail behind the manor.

"And make sure everyone stays there!" Kara added.

Emily turned to Kara. "You find Adriane and see what's going on. And play nice."

"I *can* sing, you know," Kara sniffed.

"Adriane is really talented, too." Emily said. "Besides, it's not about who's the best."

"Yeah, it's about being onstage in front of a zillion people with Johnny Conrad!" Kara exclaimed, then grumbled under her breath,. "Besides, she started it."

"It doesn't matter who started it. What's important is that the two of you work this out."

Kara frowned. "Okay. But hurry and get back and help me get this place ready. There's probably a million things to do."

Emily dashed off toward the woods following after the animals, while Kara hauled the front door open and bolted into the shadowed foyer of the manor.

"This place is always so dusty and—"

She hit the hall light switch and stopped dead in her tracks.

The manor had been transformed. WELCOME JOHNNY!

banners and band posters were everywhere, and the manor itself sparkled. Little signs with arrows and notes like THIS WAY TO THE KITCHEN, THIS WAY TO JOHNNY'S ROOM, THIS WAY TO BAND QUARTERS, THIS WAY TO REHEARSAL AREA, and many more were all over the place.

"*Adriane!*" Kara screamed, storming into the wide foyer.

A loud power chord ripped through the empty halls and echoed throughout the manor. With the volume turned up a notch, a succession of new chords barreled over Kara, bouncing around the entryway in a catchy rhythm.

Adriane was practicing her guitar already? How had she gotten the manor ready so fast? Putting all of this together must have taken days—unless, of course, she had a little magical help. And Adriane was certainly the most adept at using her magic to make things happen.

Ignoring her relief that everything seemed ready for Johnny, Kara stomped up the wide main staircase to the second floor.

Funky chords shuffled down the hallway as Kara peeked into the open doors. Every room she looked in had been thoroughly cleaned and dusted, sparkling and ready for guests.

Squealing guitar feedback echoed away into silence as Kara walked along the brightly lit corridor to the library. Then she heard something else and froze. Footsteps. From one of the rooms just ahead of her. Someone moving things around.

The lights went out, plunging the hall into darkness. Pale moonlight streamed through a small window at the end of the corridor as Kara's eyes took a moment to adjust. Suddenly, a figure sprang from the library and raced toward the window, cutting a hard left and disappearing down another corridor before Kara could get a decent glimpse.

"Hey, Miss Guitar Hero!" Kara called out.

She ran toward the window, nearly tripping on a section of rug that had been bunched up. By the time she reached the corridor's intersection, the long hallway leading down to other rooms was empty.

"Adriane, come on!" Kara yelled. She didn't have time for this. Then she noticed a weird, golden glow at her feet, making her shadow stretch far and wide before her. Turning, she saw a flickering light reaching out from the open door to the library.

"Adriane?" she called out, peering inside the library cautiously.

No one was there. The library felt oppressively silent.

Kara walked into the large circular room. Moonlight glowed through the huge picture windows, illuminating rows upon rows of books lining the walls. The panel concealing the Ravenswood computer screen was closed. Everything seemed untouched.

A shadow moved near Kara's feet. She looked up and stared at the giant mobile that hung from the center of the library's domed ceiling. It was made of a series of celestial pieces, a sun, planets with moons, comets, and stars all designed to swing in synchronous movement. It swayed lightly in the air. Had someone just hurried by it?

Moving under the mobile, she bumped into the large reading table. Rich leather-bound books with gold trim were piled high. Had Adriane been reading all these volumes?

Kara stopped. One of the old musty books lay open. A tall candle cast a wavering light upon its pages. A low, whistling breeze taunted the flame as it flowed into the room from an open window a dozen feet away.

Someone had been in here, reading this book. She looked at the ancient gold lettering along the book's spine: *The Art of Spellsinging*. What kind of research was Adriane doing?

A shuffling noise from the hall made Kara spin around again. She didn't like this game Adriane seemed to be playing one bit.

But *was* it Adriane?

She thought about calling Lyra, but Johnny and his people would be here any minute. She examined the book. She was about to close it when the wind kicked up, making the candlelight shine brightly upon one particular passage.

Song of truth, words of age
Spread in song what you read on this page
Music awakens the power of the lightbringer
For stars to shine, call upon the spellsinger

Kara stared at the passage for several long moments. The rest of the world, all her responsibilities and even her fight with Adriane, were suddenly swept away and forgotten.

The power of the lightbringer? It almost sounded like the book was talking about *her*. She was the blazing star, after all. That's what the Fairimentals said, even if none of the girls had figured out exactly what that meant. The three had been chosen to become mages, magic users. Emily was a healing mage, using the power of her rainbow jewel to help animals. Adriane was a warrior, using the magic of her wolf stone to defend the magic. But Kara hadn't found a jewel and still didn't understand her blazing star powers . . . Maybe spellsinging was the answer.

"What's that you're reading?" a familiar voice said over her shoulder.

Kara jumped and stumbled away from the table, knocking over the candle in the process. She reached for it—but Adriane was closer and quicker; the warrior snatched the candle before it could fall and set it back upright, its flame never going out.

She didn't even look at Kara. She swung her cherry-red electric guitar across her back on its black leather strap and stared at the open pages, her lips forming the words Kara had just read. "Spellsinging. That's cool . . ."

"Yeah, well, it's better than loud obnoxious power chords! That's so last century!" Kara glared daggers at

Adriane, but the warrior was oblivious. "I can't believe you are so jealous that I'm going to sing with Johnny.."

"No one said it's going to be you, Miss Center of the Universe," Adriane retorted as she scanned more pages. "Besides, I wouldn't exactly call what you do singing."

"Oh, that's so funny I forgot to laugh!"

"Didn't that Fairimental say something about spellsinging? Where did you find this book?"

Kara crossed her arms. "Oh, like you weren't so reading it before I got here!"

Adriane looked up. "I've never seen it before."

"Tell me another one." Kara paced back and forth under the mobile. "That Fairimental also said use the fairy map. How can we do that? The sorceress has it."

"If you hadn't lost it," Adriane waved her arms in frustration, "We might still have it!"

"I didn't lose it! I . . . I—*oooh!*"

"It did say you're in danger—all of us," Adriane continued.

Kara shot a withering gaze. "Well, that's your department, isn't it? Saving the day? I just have my stupid little concert to take care of, thank you very much!"

A loud *squawk* buzzed from her backpack. She fished out the walkie-talkie.

"What!" she snapped.

"Drone One to Queen—"

"Yeah, yeah, what is it?"

"Target on route to Ravenswood—"

Kara's eyes went wide as she shut off the walkie-talkie. "He's coming!" She surveyed the room frantically. There were several strange-looking objects strewn across the tables. "We have to put away anything that looks magical!"

"We can hide everything next to the computer," Adriane said, gathering up the books from the table and walking to the secret compartment. She lifted her wrist and held her amber wolf stone against the wall panel. The stone flashed with golden light, outlining the wall with bright lines. The panel silently slid back to reveal the computer screen of the Ravenswood library.

Kara tapped her foot and crossed her arms. "I don't have a jewel. How am I supposed to get in there?"

"Oh." Adriane smiled wryly. "I forgot."

Frustrated, Kara stormed across the room and started gathering items. A snow globe that was anything but what it looked like, several talismans of protection given by the wondrous creatures of Ravenswood, and a small woven dreamcatcher.

"What's the deal with all these candles?" Adriane asked. "Why didn't you just turn on a light?"

"I thought that was *your* touch. You have been, like, so busy around here," Kara retorted with a snort.

"Yeah," Adriane chuckled. "I was cleaning up the manor with Storm, but we weren't in the library—" She looked at Kara, then pointed to the books. "If you didn't find these books and I didn't—"

Kara felt a chill that had nothing to do with the cool

air filtering in through the open window. Someone else *had* been here. The person she had glimpsed in the hall hadn't been Adriane. Was that person still here?

She regarded the open window. "Someone else has been here," Kara said stiffly.

"No way," Adriane disagreed, picking up the book about spellsinging. "Storm would have warned me if someone had snuck into the manor."

Kara dumped the items she had gathered behind the secret panel. "Or some *thing* . . ." She flashed on the Fairimental's warning of danger.

"This could be very useful for my singing debut with Johnny," Adriane said, opening the book again.

Kara's entire body tensed. She was about to start screaming when something sparkled from the hiding place. Kara's eyes opened wide. It was the horn of Lorelei, the unicorn, given to Emily to lead the girls across the magic web and back home to Ravenswood. The power of the horn was supposed to grant the user *any* magic he or she desired. Kara cut a quick glimpse back at Adriane and saw that the raven-haired girl was riffling through the pages.

With one quick, furtive motion, Kara snatched the crystalline unicorn horn and slipped it in her backpack.

Emily was right, Kara decided. It didn't matter who started this business between her and Adriane—only who finished it.

In other words, whoever stood onstage with Johnny

Conrad, singing in front of the world, the envy of every-one, was the winner!

The unicorn horn sparkled with magical energy as she closed her backpack.

6

*K*ARA HEARD THE knock at the manor's front door
and only barely beat Adriane to it. She smiled
brightly as Johnny and his mix master, a dude called Inky
Toon, stepped inside. Inky was a big guy, well over six
feet tall, with ebony skin and cropped black hair. He
wore a red hoodie with oversized jeans, silver sneakers,
and a black bandana with little yellow squares. He
sported sunglasses and a blinding smile.

Johnny was, as always, totally laid-back and cool.

"Hello, paradise!" Johnny whistled as he looked
around the spacious foyer. "This place is awesome!"

Kara smiled. "Welcome to Ravenswood Manor. I'll be
happy to show you guys the digs."

"Cool crib, girl," Inky said. "You know what I say, life

is always a par-tay, and this is a place where we can work it."

Looking vexed that Kara was getting props for welcoming Johnny and his people to the manor, Adriane cleared her throat. Inky nodded toward the raven-haired girl and handed her his leather jacket. "Yo, guitar girl—hang that up for me? We got a few things out in the car, too. Thanks!"

Adriane took the jacket, adjusted the guitar still hung over her back, and walked off with it. "Yeah, sure, you're welcome . . ."

"Everyone else is on their way," Inky said.

"Everyone else?" Kara stopped in mid-grin.

"Yeah, you know what I'm sayin—we got our crew to take care of."

"Sure . . . okay, I guess."

Soon, the entire mansion was buzzing. Johnny's band and all his technical people had arrived, along with Emily and Gran. Adriane's grandmother looked concerned about the way the manor was being taken over. She even took Adriane outside for what looked like a stern talking-to.

Good, Kara thought.

The band's equipment piled up in the immense dining room, which would be used for rehearsal space. The parlor, kitchen, and adjoining sitting rooms were overflowing with the newcomers, including a reporter interviewing Mrs. Windor!

"I do *not* listen to rock and roll music," Windor was

droning on. "Big events are dangerous for a small community. Attracts all the wrong elements." She eyed the reporter suspiciously.

"All right then, thank you, Mrs. Windor." She signaled her crew to move on to Johnny.

Mrs. Windor sneered as the rock star walked past. "Ravenswood should be shut down, not saved!"

Johnny raised an eyebrow. "I'm here to support a worthwhile, charitable cause."

"You have no idea what kind of animals are *really* here!" Mrs. Windor snapped.

Kara couldn't believe what she was hearing. She had to do something!

Suddenly, Inky was sweeping in ahead of Johnny. "Come on, now, people," Inky said with a broad sweep of his big arms that forced Mrs. Windor out the front door. "Animal rights is an important issue and we're here to support *all* animals."

"Soon the whole world will know what you're hiding here!" Windor bellowed as the door closed in her face.

"Who was that?" Johnny asked Kara.

Kara flushed. "Mrs. Windor. She'll do anything to stop this concert."

Johnny chuckled. "Well, I wouldn't worry about her. Something tells me she's going to go ape over this show! Trust me." His dark eyes glittered with the bright lights held by the camera crew.

Kara smiled. Of course he was right.

"Believe it," he winked.

Someone slipped a disk in a boom box and the room filled with a hip-hop blaster that was tearing up the charts. Johnny spun around the room demonstrating some of the hot dance moves that had catapulted him to stardom. Everyone cheered and got into the groove.

Kara leaned next to Emily against the wall beside the fireplace. Johnny had a way of making her feel so relaxed. He was just *so* cool.

"What do you think of Johnny?" she asked.

Emily fluttered her hand over her heart and rolled her eyes. "He is *so* cute!"

"Back at ya!"

"Everything okay with you and Adriane?" Emily asked.

Kara tensed, suddenly thinking of the unicorn horn she had swiped. Guilt overwhelmed her at the thought of Emily finding out what she had done. But one look at Johnny and the feeling vanished. "Don't ask."

"That bad?"

"Worse." Kara remembered the book she'd found in the library—and the mysterious visitor who must have been looking it over. She told Emily about it and they quietly slipped upstairs to investigate, away from their company. They unlocked the library and went inside. Emily popped on the light. She started—and pointed at the rug. "Look!"

Kara focused on the large woven area rug by the door. The red, blue, and gold weave was splotched with brown.

"Someone tracked mud in here," Emily said. Those weren't splotches—they were footprints. Looking closer, she determined that the prints were wide, with three toes. "Only these prints are not human. Some kind of animal."

Kara and Emily exchanged worried glances. "It can't be bad," Kara said. "The dreamcatcher would have stopped it."

"That Fairimental warned us about something dangerous," Emily reminded her. "Is that the book?"

"That's it."

For an instant, Kara thought she heard someone singing in the hall. Then the sound faded and her mind filled with calm.

Deciding it was just music from downstairs, Emily and Kara read a passage from the book:

> *Spellsing as one*
> *See your work done*
> *Spellsing as three*
> *What you picture will be*

"It sounds like it's talking about us," Emily said. "The power of three."

"So spellsinging must be some kind of spell casting using music," Kara mused.

"You think whatever was in here was looking for this magic?"

"Knock, knock," a deep voice called.

Kara and Emily spun to see Johnny standing in the open doorway, leaning against the frame with his confident grin. That's weird—Kara thought she had locked the door behind them.

"What an incredible room!" Johnny eased into the library, admiring all the shelves of books and the odd little curios, all fashioned in an animal motif. "So this is the famous Ravenswood Manor library!"

Kara slapped the book closed and passed it to Emily, who slid it behind her back.

"Look at all these books!" he continued, walking around the circular room. "And these paintings are awesome! An original Parrish, a Bates, and this. . . . whoa! The Munro Orrery," he gazed up at the intricate mobile.

"Awesome," Kara agreed, totally in awe of her guest.

"How do you know so much about Ravenswood?" Emily asked.

"I'm a history-head." Johnny smiled. "Especially when it comes to haunted houses."

"Haunted houses?" Emily glanced at Kara.

"Yeah, I live for this stuff. Ravenswood and the woods around the preserve are famous: full of ghosts, witches, and monsters!" He laughed.

"The woods aren't haunted," Emily said. "That's just kids' stories."

"No? I'm sure there are some extra-special things going on here." Johnny's deep blue eyes sparkled as he smiled.

Kara nudged Emily's arm. "Maybe you should take our *homework* to Adriane."

"Yeah, good idea," Emily said, bumping into bookshelves as she edged out the door.

"Soooo," Kara said, smiling and sidling to the reading table, away from the secret computer panel. "You're a Ravenswood buff. That's cool, Johnny." Her smile faltered and her heart started racing and suddenly she felt like a complete idiot. "Johnny. I called you Johnny . . . *Can* I call you Johnny? Or should it be Mr. Conrad, or Mr. C, or—"

Johnny laughed, and it was such a friendly laugh, an almost musical sound, that it instantly calmed Kara's jitters.

"Johnny's my name, don't wear it out." The rock star smiled, turning his baby blues to the rows of books. "I love to read." He ran long fingers over the rich leather-bound volumes.

"You do?"

He laughed again and a warm, comforting breeze seemed to wash over her.

"Of course," Johnny said softly as he scanned the titles on the shelves. "I'm on the road all the time. I've got to do something to make it less boring."

"Boring?" Kara asked incredulously. "Your life, boring? I don't believe it."

He glanced her way. "Well, there are some pretty exciting moments. Like meeting new people and seeing new places . . ."

His sigh even sounded like music, and it made Kara's

heart beat like thunder. Suddenly, all she could think about was what he was going to say or do next.

"And getting up onstage," Johnny said quickly, "performing for my fans, singing my music. It's like . . . magic." He turned to face Kara, and for a split second she caught a flash of fire in his eyes.

Kara took a step back. She felt feverish. This was unreal. *She* was getting to spend time alone with Johnny Conrad!

Just wait until she told Heather and Molly and Tiff about this . . . she had the sudden impulse to sing it to the world!

"So you're a singer, too," Johnny said brightly.

Kara was startled. "Huh?"

"Your dad told me you were dying to win the contest, you and your pal with the guitar. Though, I hope for her sake that she's got one top-notch voice, 'cause you've got her way beat where it counts."

Kara nearly choked. "I do? R—r—really?"

"I know about these things," he said, low, musical tones seeming to echo beneath each of his words . . . words that filled her with the same confidence that radiated from the singer. "You've got something special. I can feel it. You know what that is?"

Kara thought of the unicorn horn . . . No, that was crazy. Johnny didn't have anything to do with magic.

"Star power," he answered for her. "And I'm never wrong."

Before Kara could even think of what to say, Inky and two others were in the doorway.

"Wow. What a spread!" Inky commented, taking in the vast library. "This place rocks!"

"Come on, Johnny, press is waiting," one of the others said, popping her gold and pink-haired head into the room. "We promised you'd do more interviews."

"Okay," Johnny said, walking to the door. He turned back and gave Kara a wink. "Star power," he repeated.

As Johnny and his crew hurried off, she felt her head start to clear and realized she'd have to be more careful in the future. This library had to remain off-limits to visitors. And there was the computer, which held secrets practically beyond imagining.

She locked the door on her way out.

Star power! Kara beamed. "Finally, someone notices!"

LATE THAT NIGHT, an exhausted Emily dropped onto her bed without even bothering to change into pajamas. She wanted to read more of the book she had taken from the mansion . . . What little she had read about spellsinging had completely captured her imagination. Magic spell casting with music—awesome!

She had to learn more, but she was so tired.

What a day this had been—and things were only going to get more exciting. It would all be wonderful, absolutely perfect—if only Kara and Adriane could work out their differences.

Then again, there was that warning from the Fairimental. If the Dark Sorceress had set another of her plots in motion, she sure had good timing. The mages were so busy and distracted now that Johnny was at Ravenswood, they hardly had time for anything else. Emily decided tomorrow they would have to get Kara to call the dragonflies. They would contact Zach on Aldenmor and find out what was happening there.

Clank!

Slam!

"Cheep-cheep!"

Emily bolted upright in bed. Those sounds had come from outside. She ran to the window and looked out at the converted barn behind their house.

"Eeep-eep-ooooook!"

Krrrrang!

Someone was in the Pet Palace.

Emily burst from her bedroom, zoomed downstairs, and headed toward the back door.

"Emily?" her mom called out. Carolyn had been downstairs in her office with the reporter who had been at Ravenswood. The reporter wanted an animal special-ist's viewpoint on the Ravenswood Preserve.

"Just checking on Dr. McHenrys monkeys," Emily called out as she whizzed by.

She ran across the small expanse of yard and entered

the Pet Palace. Bizarre! Some old woman was prying open the cages that held the former circus monkeys and letting them go free!

"Hey!" Emily hollered.

The old woman turned and Emily froze. Fear ripped up her spine, tickling the hairs on her neck. Mrs. Windor's eyes glowed with red fire. She was hunched over, slobbering like a wild animal. A long tongue wagged from her mouth as saliva dripped to the wooden floor. A sudden burst of white light filled the space. For a moment, Emily didn't know what had happened—then she saw her mother appear outside the nearby open window and saw the reporter with a flash camera.

Dr. Carolyn Fletcher's jaw dropped. "What's going on in here? What are you—"

The photographer snapped another shot, his flash blinding mother and daughter.

"Yiiieeeee-eeek-eeek-eeek!"

The monkeys howled and hooted, the sudden flash making them leap from the top of one cage to another. One landed on Mrs. Windor's back and clung to her as she raced off.

Screaming madly, Mrs. Windor flung herself past the astonished trio and out the door, running across the backyard toward the parks and playing fields. The monkeys followed: one flying through the window and knocking the photographer flat on his back before bounding off into the darkness, another racing around and leading Emily and her mother in circles before escaping through the open back door.

Emily and her mother went outside, just in time to see the photographer drive off in his car.

"What was *that* all about?" Emily's mom asked, startled.

Emily knew Mrs. Windor wanted to disrupt the concert any way she could and to prove the animals here weren't safe. But this was crazy! And the way Mrs. Windor had looked—almost as if she weren't human. A cold chill lodged in her spine.

Shaking her head, Emily said, "I guess Mrs. Windor finally went over the edge."

They went back inside to grab flashlights so they could hunt for the missing monkeys.

Flashing red eyes gleamed from the edge of the woods, watching their house carefully. Mrs. Windor hummed a strange little song and backed into the shadows.

The monkeys followed her, their heads lolling, their eyes glazed, completely entranced by the melody.

Then, suddenly, Mrs. Windor bent low and hissed at the animals, her features melting and changing, her skin turning green and scaly, her eyes morphing to smoldering yellow slits in the night, her teeth sharpening to nasty points.

The monkeys shrieked and ran off in terror as the creature that used to be Beasley Windor straightened to its full seven foot form, its long arms swaying, its claws clicking and clacking in the near dark. It leaned back its massive head and roared.

Across the expanse of woods, deep in the heart of Ravenswood, cries of fear erupted in the magic glade. Magical animals that had been sleeping soundly suddenly awoke, horrified by the presence they sensed: a creature, dank and foul, from the darkest depths of their nightmares. And it was here.

7

*T*HE MORNING SUN cast deep, long shadows behind Kara as she trudged along the high, grassy bank of the Chitakaway River, head down, feet dragging. She swung her backpack by its straps, letting it graze the dewy grass and earth, not even caring if it got stained. Sparkling water danced over wide flat stones jutting from the river, the roaring and rushing creating its own special music.

She had suffered the most restless night's sleep she could possibly have imagined. At one moment flying high in amazing dreams of success, basking in the glow of superstardom, the envy of all her friends—and at the next moment tossed into throes of anxiety, running scared in the blackest nightmares of failure, feeling utter humiliation as everyone laughed at her, their jeers and snickers echoing in her mind.

"Okay, okay, just breathe," Kara said aloud, painfully aware of her own shortcomings as a singer—and the event looming over her this evening. The preliminary, karaoke-style audition for the big contest would be held at seven in the school auditorium. Inky Toon would pick five lucky finalists who'd be allowed to sing during the preshow on Saturday. Johnny would judge that round of competition personally.

Kara would have to sing in front of dozens of people tonight—maybe even hundreds . . . including Adriane.

She clutched her backpack tighter, tormented by indecision. She could feel the unicorn horn inside, radiating with power, calling to her. Yet she also felt a nagging twinge of guilt for taking it in the first place, and for what she planned to do with it.

The whole concert was supposed to be about helping Ravenswood, and Kara had organized the benefit like a pro. But when it came to magic, she was a total amateur. Emily and Adriane had found their gems months ago and were constantly working to expand and control their abilities. So while her friends were on their way to becoming real mages, she was left behind, unable to control powers she didn't understand. The only thing she knew for sure was that she supercharged Emily and Adriane's jewels. But why should she, Kara Davies, play the role of helper? Why didn't she have a jewel of her own, something to *prove* that she was the blazing star?

If she was ever going to become a real mage, she had to use a jewel. A shiver passed through her; the unicorn horn practically buzzed with a vibrant life all its own. So why not this? With trembling fingers, Kara opened the backpack and touched the unicorn horn. Sparks of energy ran around the intricate scalloped shape, sparkling over her fingers.

A fluttering in the breeze behind her made her turn just in time to see Lyra descend. Kara marveled at the cat's powerful magic wings. Unlike the feathery butterfly-shaped wings of a pegasus, Lyra's were sleek, hawk-like, built for speed and fast maneuvering. The tapered, golden wings folded to the cat's sides, flashed, and disappeared.

"*No ride this morning?*" Lyra asked, brushing up against Kara's hip.

Kara scratched the cat behind the ears and shrugged. "I decided to walk."

"*Storm and I checked the entire preserve. We've found no sign of the intruder that scared the animals last night.*"

"Maybe it was just a nightmare," Kara said.

"*Then we all had the same nightmare.*"

"But nothing bad can slip through the dreamcatcher."

"*Unless it came from somewhere else. With all the people starting to arrive in Ravenswood, we're on high alert.*"

"Okay." Kara looked down, shuffling her feet.

"*Are you still concerned about this singing contest?*"

"No! Yes. Maybe. . . ."

"You sounded good the other morning."

"Yeah, its easy when you have a band like Be*Tween to sing along with. Tonight I have to sing all by myself!"

"You're making too much out of this." Lyra nudged her flank playfully against Kara, hard enough to make the girl wobble for a second before regaining her footing.

"Quit it! I am not! The entire school is going to be there!"

As they neared the Saddleback Bridge that would take Kara over the river and onto the main road to school, Lyra stopped and sat back on her haunches.

"Okay, let's hear," Lyra said.

"What, now?" Kara stopped, irritated.

"Give it your best shot," the cat said patiently.

Kara looked around. A few blackbirds sat in an ancient oak. Other than the birds, the area was empty.

She took a breath. "Okay, you asked for it." She put down her backpack and struck her best superstar pose.

She hummed a bit and started her choreographed steps, adding a few new ones she picked up watching Johnny and his crew.

Lyra bobbed her head along. *"Good moves, but can you sing a little louder?"*

Kara went for it.

The blackbirds screamed in protest at the obnoxious, screeching voice that suddenly interrupted their day. They flew away, squawking back a few insults.

Lyra listened patiently. Kara couldn't tell if the cat was smiling or about to hurl a furball.

"Well?"

Lyra sat for a second then stretched her back and stood. "*Well . . .*"

"I knew it." Kara swept up her backpack and stomped off. "I stink!"

Lyra caught up to her. "*I wouldn't say that.*"

"Well, what would you say?"

"*You just need a little help.*"

"Exactly what I was thinking!" Kara looked relieved as she held up her backpack.

"*A few lessons with the singing coach and some practice.*"

"Oh—yeah . . ." Kara lowered the backpack.

Lyra cocked her head. "*What were you thinking?*"

"Uh . . . I should practice with the choir," she said, embarrassed now to admit what she was *really* thinking about.

They headed across the pedestrian bridge. Beyond it, the trail to school wound past the orchards. Kara knew that Lyra would have to turn back once they got there, or else risk drawing attention. That meant if Kara wanted to tell Lyra what was on her mind, she'd have to do it quickly.

"Lyra, have you ever done something you know you really shouldn't have? Something a part of you wishes you could take back, while another part of you is saying, 'hey, I'd do it again.'"

The cat's eyes narrowed. *"Why are you asking?"*

Kara looked away. If she told Lyra about the unicorn horn, then she'd never be able to keep it; she'd feel too guilty about making her friend an accomplice after the fact.

"This thing you're talking about," Lyra prompted, *"it can't be undone?"*

It occurred to Kara that she could go to the manor *right now* and put the unicorn horn back where it belonged. No one would ever know she'd taken it in the first place.

But . . . she needed it. How could she hope to compete in the contest *without* using magic? Magic that had been given to the girls. Well, to Emily actually. But it had been given to help all three of them.

"She's your friend," Lyra said. *"I think you should just talk to her."*

"Huh?" Kara asked, startled.

"Adriane's just stubborn, unlike someone else I know," the cat said, rubbing playfully against Kara's side.

"Yeah," Kara said, quickly recovering from her surprise. "She should be apologizing to me!"

Lyra sighed.

"I've got to get to school!" Kara rushed ahead, anxious to get away from Lyra before she was forced to look her friend in the eye—she knew she couldn't do that—and tell a lie, even a little white lie like pretending she meant Adriane all along.

∞

Kara couldn't concentrate on classwork. At lunch she only barely heard Emily as the girl went on about the craziness with Mrs. Windor the night before, which, thanks to the picture-snapping reporter, was even more fully reported in the morning edition of the Stonehill Gazette. At least that was one problem solved. No one was going to believe Windor now about what she had seen in the woods.

But Kara's greatest frustration was that she didn't have the spellsinging book. If she had been more on top of things, she would have gotten it back from Emily the night before. The time spent with Johnny had seemed to cast another kind of a spell on her, making her feel light-headed with joy, not able to think as clearly as she usually did. Today she could hardly concentrate. All she could think about was spellsinging. And Johnny.

Kara barely paid attention as Heather, Molly, and Tiffany crowded around her, wanting to know all the details about Johnny Conrad. She was the "center of the universe," as Adriane had put it, just like she wanted to be . . . but for how long?

It was time to do something.

∞

KARA MARCHED TOWARD the music building and stopped—then leaped behind a large maple tree. Every time she tried to enter the music room, she couldn't. She was too scared to make the move. Peering around the tree, she saw the open doors that led from the music room to the track behind the school.

She listened to the uplifting voices of the school's choir practicing in the spacious music room. They sounded so rich and beautiful. A soloist took the lead and Kara sang along, desperately attempting to match the girl's incredible voice. But every note Kara sang was either flat or sharp, early or late, always somehow just plain wrong. Even when she tried the easier route of singing along with the rest of the choir, she was never once in tune with them.

Kara tried to belt it out like she did when singing along to Be*Tween. A few stray dogs ran around the tree, barking. She quickly shut her mouth, looking around. The last thing she needed was for someone to hear her voice before the big contest.

For a moment, she thought about just giving up. Then she thought of Adriane's triumphant smile, the one she'd give her when Kara backed out.

No, she *had* to sing at the contest tonight. She had to make it to the final round and prove to Adriane that she was . . . that she was a star—the blazing star!

Johnny thought she was special, and he should know.

She opened her backpack and took out the unicorn horn. The crystalline horn shone in the afternoon sun, rainbow sparkles running up and down its delicate spiraled curves.

"I want to sing like a star!" Kara said.

She held it tight and tried a chorus of "Supernatural High."

It wasn't working—she sounded exactly the same. Kara felt close to panicking. This was her last hope. What was she doing wrong? Maybe the horn worked just for Emily.

I need to focus, like Emily and Adriane do when they use their stones, she thought.

Think musical magic. Magic to make music. Music to make magic. She thought of the book she had found in the library. The strange words of spellsinging drifted in her mind like tinkling bells.

Spellsing as one
And see your work done

"Okay . . ." Kara whispered. Spellsinging. A musical spell could help focus magic. How hard could it be?

I want to sing like a bird
The best in the world
Make my voice ring
I'm super-stylin'

Cute, she thought. Not too bad for her first magic spell.

She tried saying the words again, but nothing happened. Then she tried singing them in a rapping rhythm, the unicorn horn clutched tightly in her hand. Suddenly, she felt wind kick up, sending a swirl of magical energy around her, lifting her long blonde hair.

Whoa!

It stopped the moment she fell silent.

Kara tried the spell again, singing the words a little more loudly now, with more confidence and control—and somehow, even though she wasn't singing what the choir was singing, she was in tune with them, her rhythms in sync, her notes flowing perfectly with theirs.

She felt the horn trembling in her hands as it focused her magic.

An ember of brilliant light suddenly flared from the horn. Kara leaped back, scared. She watched in amazement as the light spread between her fingers, swirling around her hands. The air felt heavy as sparkling diamond magic raced up her arms and swirled around her. Her heart thundered in a chorus of power.

Yes! The jewel was exactly what she needed. Just like the last time, the exquisite power she used with the jewel of the unicorn. Only this time it was stronger—just what she needed to change—

This was wrong! She knew it and fought against its call, but another part of her sang with the harmonies of her magic. *Her magic!* The power was exhilarating. The

wind screamed in her ears, whipping around her in a cyclone of magically charged air.

Her entire form blazed diamond bright as the magic crackled across her skin. The power seemed so much larger than her small frame. How could it stay contained? And once released, how could she control it?

Taking a deep breath, she cleared her mind of anything but the flows and ebbs of the magic. In a few heartbeats, the glow simmered then grew back to an intense blaze. She could do this!

Kara squeezed her eyes closed and centered her breathing. With a certainty that rocked her world, she locked the magic to her will.

Kara started to sing. A perfect A note rang from her mouth. She moved to C and F sharp then began running up the scale, notes perfectly in tune, each rising in perfect pitch. Her control was incredible. Her voice became a lilting, wondrous sound, cascading like sweet summer rain as it moved up and down the scale.

The horn blazed with power. The magic inside of her sang for release.

Kara was ready.

She raced up three octaves and with perfect breath control, she hit a triple high C.

The tree trunk burst with an explosive *crack!*

Waves of invisible force rippled from the horn—and a window shattered in the school!

She heard the choir screaming in surprise.

Kara gasped as she wrestled the magic under control—but somewhere deep inside, somewhere she feared to look too closely, a part of her cackled with wicked delight. A flicker of a smile fluttered around her mouth. The magic was hers.

"YOU CAN GO now, Mrs. Windor," the desk sergeant said as he opened the cell door.

"It's about time!" Mrs. Windor clutched a rolled up copy of the Stonehill Gazette, revealing the photograph of her at the Pet Palace, a monkey on her back. "I was nowhere near that house!"

The sergeant looked at her warily. He was a big man with salt and pepper hair. "Uh-huh. Beside the pictures, there were three eyewitness accounts. The photographer, Dr. Fletcher, and her daughter . . ."

"All of them at Ravenswood are in on this together. I bet it was that Nakoda who dressed up as me for these clearly *staged* photographs!"

"Ah," the officer said. "And why would she do that?"

"To discredit me, of course. I know what they're hiding there! Monsters, I tell you!"

The desk sergeant said, "I'm just stating the facts, ma'am. Now why don't you go home, cool off, and have a nice long rest? You might even consider seeing a . . . doctor."

"That was not me last night!" Mrs. Windor shrieked as she nervously backed out of the building.

The desk sergeant was no longer listening. Instead, he was watching to see if the door might be kind enough to hit Mrs. Windor in the rear end on her way out.

"Whaaaah!" she yelped.

He chuckled as it did.

8

*T*HE CHAOS CAUSED by Kara's accidental window shattering blew over pretty fast. No one had been hurt, but a lot of students were badly shaken by the sudden "windstorm."

The worst of it was that Kara *knew* she should feel terrible about what she had done—but she didn't. She carefully tested her new vocal proficiency as she walked down the hallway. Humming a tune under her breath, she heard a familiar light musical ringing and felt a tingling throughout her body. After what happened outside, she couldn't risk anything louder. She was dying to find out how long the effects would last. As soon as she could get free, she had to find a secluded area to do further tests.

She just had to force herself to make it through the rest of the school day.

Finally, the three o'clock bell sounded and Kara rushed to her locker. All around her, kids were buzzing with excitement over the karaoke contest. Kara ignored them all, collecting her backpack and her books as fast as she could.

"Hey!"

She looked up to see Adriane standing there, glaring at her.

"Hey is for horses."

"You haven't said one word to me or Emily today, and now you're rushing off again!" Adriane said angrily. The wolf stone on Adriane's wrist suddenly pulsed with hot light as Kara lifted her backpack from her locker. Adriane quickly covered her wrist with the sleeve of her jacket.

She leaned in close and hissed, "Aren't you even the least bit concerned about what happened to the animals last night?"

"No, should I be?"

"They think some kind of monster might have gotten through the dreamcatcher," Adriane whispered, glancing around to make sure no one else was listening.

"A monster *can't* get through. That's the whole point, duh!"

"We need to get a message to Zach," Adriane insisted, referring to the human boy she had met on Aldenmor who'd been raised by mistwolves. "Maybe he found the Fairy Glen."

"And how do you propose we do that?"

"We can use the portal or the d-flies—"

"We can't open the portal, and now you want a long-distance dragonfly call to Aldenmor? That's the *last* thing I need right now!"

"And just where were you when that 'windstorm' hit?" Adriane asked suspiciously, rubbing her gemstone as if it irritated her.

"Uh . . . getting stuff done . . ." Kara held the backpack behind her, as far away from Adriane's wrist as she could.

"What has gotten into you?" Adriane demanded.

"*Me?* What about you, Miss I'm-So-Gonna-Sing-With-Johnny!"

"Yeah, okay, I got a little carried away. But I'm over that."

"Tell me another one."

"Look, you have to get this concert back under control. Gran is getting really annoyed."

"You were the one who put Johnny and his people at Ravenswood. Don't come crying to me!" Kara pointed out.

"This is *your* show, superstar! You need to get over to Ravenswood right now and finalize a million details."

"I can't . . . I . . . I'm busy."

Adriane's eyebrow rose. "With what?"

"I'm going to . . ." Guilt flashed through her. There might be something dangerous at the preserve. The girls had no idea what was going on in Aldenmor. They needed to talk to Zach. And there *were* a million details to deal with before the concert.

Kara sighed. All she really wanted to do was lose herself in the dream of Johnny and her sharing the spotlight, singing before a crowd, basking in their love—

Shouts and screams broke her thoughts. Hundreds of kids were suddenly pouring out the front door of the school.

What now? Kara thought as she followed and bolted from the building.

Suddenly, everyone turned to look at her. Silence fell as the crowd parted like a sea to reveal a long black limo parked by the curb. Johnny leaned on the car's trunk, grinning as the horde of fans flocked around him.

Laughing, he signed notebooks, articles of clothing, even one kid's arm. Then he turned and looked right at Kara.

"Good luck with the contest, everyone. We'll be seeing you all at the show tomorrow." He raised a fist into the air. "Ravenswood!" he shouted.

"Johnny!" the crown yelled back. "Johnny!"

"Let's hear it for the other star of this concert. The one responsible for the entire show," Johnny said, holding out his hand in Kara's direction. Kara walked through the crowd in a daze.

Johnny opened the rear door for Kara to climb in. "Your coach awaits, princess. Where to?"

"Home is cool."

He hopped to the other side, and in seconds they were off.

Kara was startled at the cheers and cries from behind them, and shocked when she looked back at the expressions on the faces of so many kids; they were calling Kara's name just as often as Johnny's. Many looked at her with the same awe they had reserved for the singer.

From the corner of her eye, she glanced at Adriane yelling something. Ooo, she must be so jealous! Smiling to herself, Kara turned and settled back in her seat.

"You know, anyone who tells you it isn't fun being a star is either lying or crazy." Johnny smiled as they drove on, heading toward a scenic road that skirted the woods and fields surrounding Stonehill.

Kara nodded. For a moment, *she* had been the one so many people were looking at with adoration . . .

"But I'm not a star, I mean, like you are," she said self-consciously.

"Don't be so modest," he said. "You put this whole show together. Everyone in this town knows you're special."

That pretty much was true, Kara thought. Not to brag, but the facts spoke for themselves. She'd been the most popular girl in school even before all this stuff with the concert started.

"The way I figure it, sometimes that light's already there, inside a person," Johnny mused.

"What light?" Kara asked.

"The light that makes someone shine like a star. The only difference between the people who make it and those who don't is doing whatever it takes to make the whole world see that light."

Kara raised her chin and tossed back her golden hair. "I want to make the whole world see what I'm about."

"There you go," Johnny said, his voice once again sounding like music, a perfect, enchanting song that made her feel better about everything. She felt more confident than she had in days. She had done the right thing taking the horn. She knew that now.

Johnny continued, "You've got to play to win. And why take the long road around if someone's pointing out a shortcut?"

Thinking about the karaoke contest, Kara couldn't have agreed more.

Cool as it was listening to him, being with him, Kara had something more urgent to do. She had to practice for the audition! Luckily, Johnny had to get back to Ravenswood for a round of interviews. She asked to be dropped off near the orchard. She could walk from there.

Johnny signaled to the driver and the limo stopped by the side of the road.

Kara smiled as she hopped out of the car. "Thanks for the ride."

"Anytime," Johnny said, rummaging in a bag. "Wait . . . Here, take this."

He placed a small locket on a slim gold chain in Kara's hands.

"I was given this before my first big show. It brought me luck." He shrugged. "Now you can use it to bring *you* luck."

"Wow. Thanks." Kara clutched the locket in her hand. She felt like she could have anything she wanted.

"I thought you might like to have it with you for the first round tonight. Not that I think you'll need it—I know you're gonna knock everyone out."

You've never even heard me sing, Kara thought, suddenly horrified. Then she relaxed. After all, she had the unicorn horn; plus, she was learning about spellsinging, her secret weapon. And the locket sealed the deal.

Her sudden confidence must have shown on her face, because Johnny winked at her. Then the limo headed off down the country road.

Kara slipped the locket around her neck. She would wear it forever!

She crossed the orchard to the pedestrian bridge that spanned the Chitakaway River. The oaks and maples were so thick on both sides, she knew no one would see or hear her practicing. The beautiful suspension bridge arced like a web over the waters flowing in the ravine far below. She set off across, feeling the bridge gently sway under her feet. About halfway across, she stopped and looked around. She was alone. Taking a breath, she tried a simple scale.

Kara's hands flew to her mouth in shock as her voice screeched across the ravine. Whatever happened before wasn't happening now. She tried three more times, but her singing sounded worse than ever. What was she going to do? How would Johnny react when he heard her voice for the first time and it wasn't as wonderful as he thought it would be?

Opening her backpack, she took out the horn. She felt the energy already sparking in her hands as she held the horn out in front of her. The magic of the unicorn was just what she needed to jump-start her spell!

> *Make my voice ring loud and clear*
> *Change how I sing, change what they hear*
> *I'll be as perfect as can be*
> *Everyone will want to sing like me*

Bright magic flashed from the horn, encircling her in twinkling diamond light. She felt the winds kick up, the bridge tremble lightly, then pulse like a backbeat. Johnny's locket sparkled and her fear melted away into pure anticipation and excitement. Power surged forth from the horn, but this time she was ready.

She opened her mouth and tried again.

Her voice rang out across the river in waves of sonic bliss. She sang perfectly in tune, every word as perfect as she had heard it on the Be*Tween song. Tapping her feet to the rhythm, Kara started to dance on the bridge. Arms moving in a tight routine, she felt light as air, dancing in the diamond white glow of unicorn magic.

A dark shadow passed overhead. Kara spun and the bridge swayed. Still in step, she looked up at fluffy white clouds rolling under a blue-domed sky. She continued her singing. No one had a chance against her style. She was *super*-stylin'!

Bump!

The bridge lunged sideways, throwing Kara off balance. Something had knocked into it from underneath. Underneath? She was at least ten stories in the air. She held the rope railing as the bridge settled, and peered over. Far below, the river ran fast, cascading over rocks and sending sprays of water high into the air.

Kara began to get an uneasy feeling in the pit of her stomach and slipped the unicorn horn into her backpack. She was about to start for the far side of the bridge when the shadow passed over again. She whipped her head up and squinted against the sun. Something big was flying right toward her. Then she saw familiar golden wings and spotted fur. She let out her breath.

"Geez, Lyra, you scared me half to death!"

The cat angled low over the far side of the bridge and swooped straight at her, coming in fast.

"What's with you?" Kara slipped her arms into her backpack. She looked up just as Lyra rammed into her, sending Kara flying backwards, the wind knocked out of her.

"Lyra!" she sputtered, shaken to the core. "What are you doing?"

Kara tried to get back on her feet but Lyra was too quick. The cat smashed into her back and Kara slammed face-first against the railing. She found herself staring straight down at the rushing river below.

Kara was too astonished to even think. Cold fear rushed up her body as she scrambled back—just as the cat roared and lunged for her again. Sharp claws raked down her side, tearing out patches of suede and silk.

"*Lyra!*" Kara screamed, flailing her arms to keep razor claws from slicing at her neck and face. "Stop it!"

The cat brutally swiped at the girl, sending Kara hurtling toward the other side. The rope caught her stomach, almost flipping her completely over. She clung to the railing, her sweater ripped, a ragged gash down her left leg.

"Please! Lyra, don't hurt me!" she cried out. Sweeping sweat-streaked hair from her face, she tried to scramble across the bridge. The riverbank was only a few dozen yards away and the path to her house just beyond it.

Lyra landed on the bridge, blocking Kara's way. The cat crouched, the fur on her flanks upright, her eyes dark with cold fire. Baring razor teeth, the cat advanced.

Tears streaming down her face, Kara searched her friend's eyes, looking for an answer. "I didn't mean to lie to you."

Lyra stared at Kara as if the girl were a hated enemy.

"I took the horn . . . I'm sorry." Kara felt as if a hole

had opened in her chest where her heart had once been. She watched Lyra snarl viciously as the beast pounced!

The girl instinctively threw her backpack in front of her. Sharp teeth sank into the pack like a vise and diamond fire exploded around the cat's head. Lyra wailed, shaking her head in pain. The pack tumbled to the ground.

Kara staggered to her feet. The unicorn horn was in her hand, blazing with power.

Feral eyes, flaring bright with hatred, turned to the girl.

"Don't make me do this!" Kara shrieked. Diamond fire ran up and down her arms, encircling her.

The cat opened her great wings and rose into the air, razor claws fully extended. With a terrifying roar, she attacked.

"*No!*" Kara screamed, forcing every ounce of will into the horn. Magic fire leaped free and crashed into the cat. For a second Lyra was held frozen in the air, seared by intense, burning magic.

Something ripped open inside Kara, a deep, bitter pain, screaming for release. She couldn't stop it. She strained, trying to pull back the power, but it streamed out of her, slamming into the cat.

For a breathless heartbeat, Kara waited. The wet thud as the cat's body hit sent spasms of sickness racking through her. She couldn't breathe. She wished she would faint. She wanted cool blackness to envelop her, to take her away from the nightmare.

Her heart thundered in her ears as she stumbled to her

feet and raced for the trees beyond the riverbank. Kara strained her muscles until they burned and felt like they might tear apart inside her body.

She burst out of the grove, her heart racing, her breath coming in ragged gasps.

Lyra! What had happened? How could she have been so viciously attacked by the one creature on the planet she trusted most?

And now Lyra was dead—killed by her best friend!

At last she fell into her empty house, her eyes burning, and raced upstairs to her room. All she wanted was to hide forever from the blackness that welled inside, threatening to devour her.

She flung open the door to her bedroom—and froze.

Lyra lay on her bed, amid a pile of stuffed animals and the mad mess of papers and pamphlets for the concert. Her eyes were closed. The cat was *snoring!*

Kara backed away in fear as Lyra's head lazily rose from the pillow. The cat yawned. "*I feel so strange. It's not like me to take a catnap.*"

Kara's back hit the door—and she gasped as she accidentally knocked it shut. "Get away from me!"

Lyra struggled up from the bed, her limbs seemingly heavy with sleep. She looked at Kara with wide, confused eyes. "*Kara, what's happened to you? You're hurt!*"

"Just go!" Kara yelled. "Go!"

Lyra bounded from the bed. "*I don't understand. Did I do something—*"

Kara's chest rose and fell with terror as she slumped to the rug, hands covering her face. "Get out! I don't ever want to see you again!"

Lyra sailed past her, giving one last look of worry and hurt before she leaped out the window. Kara slammed the window shut—and locked it.

Then she collapsed on her bed, clutching the locket that had miraculously not been lost at the bridge.

She cried for a very long time.

BY THE RUSHING waters of the river, a second winged cat carefully pulled its broken body onto the damp earth. It shook its head and cried out in pain. Then, in a single fluid movement, the creature changed. Animal limbs extended, bones reshaped and straightened, becoming long, human legs. Gashes healed as claws turned into fingers. Fur retreated into flesh.

Johnny Conrad stood—or the creature that looked like Conrad.

So it was true. The girl wielded the power of a unicorn horn. The Dark Sorceress had warned him it might be here. Considering the forces he had seen Kara unleash on the bridge, there could be little doubt about the girl's ability to do what was required.

Keep Kara under his spell. Keep her confused enough so she only trusted him—that was the plan. He had only been able to use a subtle spell on the warrior—the girl's mistwolf was already getting suspicious—but it had been enough. The stunt with Windor took care of that problem. Now he had taken care of the flying cat before the animal could sense the spell on her bonded, but still, the other animals knew he was here. He had to move fast. It was time to drive the final wedge between the warrior and the blazing star.

And when the moment was right, Kara would use her magic to align the portals hidden in the fairy map—and the pathway to Avalon would be revealed.

Spellsinging was the perfect way to control the blazing star's magic. That book had been meant for Kara alone, but the other mages now knew of it.

Perhaps he could use this to his advantage.

After all, evil wore many faces—and the Skultum could wear any he desired.

9

$\mathcal{E}$VENING HAD FALLEN and Kara had pulled herself together as best she could. She had been lucky;
none of the wounds were deep. She bandaged her leg
and cleaned the scratches on her arms and sides. She
had to tell Emily and Adriane, but she didn't know what
to say. It still made no sense. She hid her feelings from
Heather, Tiffany, and Molly, who had dropped by with
a triple-cheese pizza to help with the concert prepara-
tions. They had no clue that Kara's world was coming
apart at the seams.

Trying to pretend everything was normal, Kara went
into overdrive. She made a grand show of flaunting the
locket Johnny had given her, regaling her friends with
stories of Johnny and his infinite wonder. She was the

fearless leader; she pushed away all the confusion she felt by talking non-stop about the details for Saturday's show, trying her hardest to pretend that her closest friend hadn't tried to rip her to shreds.

While Kara sorted through a pile of papers, talking about ticket takers, additional parking, concession stands, placement of banners, and a hundred other things, Heather drifted over to the window and ran through a few simple voice exercises.

Kara kept talking until Tiff and Molly shushed her into silence. When Heather was done, they stared at her in shock.

"That was *amazing!*" Tiffany exclaimed.

"You've been holding out on us, girl!" Molly applauded.

They're right, Kara thought. She had never realized how beautiful Heather's voice was.

"How long have you been singing?" Kara asked, looking away and trying to sound like it was no big deal.

"No big thing," Heather said modestly, pulling her long red hair back in a ponytail. "You know my mom used to sing, and it gives us something to do together at church."

"Well, tomorrow you're singing at the church of Johnny Conrad!" Tiffany quipped.

Heather blushed. "You think I really have a chance?"

Tiffany swiveled her hips and shimmied into a dance step. "*Let me tell you, if I sing it true, get up and start the dance,*" she sang, imitating Johnny.

Molly jumped to her friend's side and sang the next verse. "*A rock-and-roll rap with some zap, come on now and take a chance.*"

The three girls sang the third verse together. "*No matter what you do it's your life, you're you.*"

They circled Kara and pushed her between them. "*So come on and take a chance and dance!*"

"*Dance, dance, dance! Take a chance and dance!*" They chanted, hopping and dancing around the room. "Cut it out!" Kara said, annoyed. She couldn't help thinking of the way she and Lyra had played together in the same way just the other morning.

"Oh, Johnny!" Molly, Tiffany, and Heather collapsed on the bed in a giggle fit, sending pizza remains flying everywhere.

Only Kara wasn't laughing.

Watching them, Kara felt a sudden flash of jealousy. Heather had natural talent. She could really sing while Kara had to resort to magic. She had borrowed, no—let's get real—*stolen* the unicorn horn.

It was wrong! Or was it . . . ?

She clutched Johnny's pendant and felt it sparkle with her magic.

I don't care if Heather is better than me, Kara thought. She doesn't want it as much as I do. She doesn't deserve it like I do . . .

"C'mon, Heather," Molly squealed. "Sing 'Supernatural High,' Be*Tween's song."

Come on, Heather, Kara mimicked Molly in her mind. Heather started singing.

> *I'm in my moon phase, my pink days*
> *When everything is okay*
> *I am beautiful, invincible*
> *Perfectly impossible*

Kara wished the girl would stop. That was *her* special song. The one she sang with Lyra!

Tiff and Molly barely seemed to notice Kara's distress.

Kara cleared her throat. "*I'm* going over to see Johnny rehearse tomorrow, and then we're doing a radio interview, then Johnny and me, we're gonna—"

Kara had to stop talking as Heather nailed another perfect note.

I can't take anymore, Kara thought. Turning away, her hands over her ears, she shouted, "Heather, will you please stop that noise? It's making me sick!"

Heather stared at Kara in shock. Tiffany and Molly also fell silent.

"Noise?" Heather asked, clearly upset.

"Sick?" Tiffany said, springing to her feet and facing Kara. "I'll tell you what's sickening! Hearing you go on and on about how tight you are with Johnny!"

"*Noise* is all the hot air that's been coming out of you ever since this whole concert thing started!" Molly added.

"This concert thing," Kara repeated, rolling her eyes. "It's *only* to save Ravenswood! Geez. You're all involved in that."

"For you," Molly said in a low, soft voice, shaking her head of short dark hair.

"Yeah," Tiffany said. "My dad says it's no big deal if those animals get shipped off to a zoo or a *professionally* run preserve. It might even be better for them."

"And sometimes it can be a little scary, giving tours with that wolf and that big cat wandering around," Heather noted.

Kara stiffened. "Fine!" she yelled, scattering the entire pile of papers against the wall with a wide swing of her hand. She couldn't bear to think about the way Lyra had attacked her today. She could still smell the sweet scent of the cat in her room—and she burst into tears.

"Kara, are you all right?" Molly asked.

Kara gave a sharp nod, quickly wiping her eyes. "If you three have better things to do, then don't let me stop you."

Heather picked up the papers and gently handed them back to Kara. "Here. We'd better go."

Kara grabbed the papers and turned away. "Like I said, there's the door. It's not hard to figure out how it works."

Heather pinned Kara with her intense gaze. "Ever since you got involved with Ravenswood, you've changed, Kara! I wish we never heard of Ravenswood!"

Kara felt like she was watching through someone else's

eyes as her friends filed out of the room. They were all turning their backs on her! Or was she sending them away?

She slammed the door shut. "Fine. I can do this without you. I don't need anyone!"

A moment later, a knock came at the door.

Ha, Kara thought. That didn't take long.

She was certain that she would find Heather and the girls looking upset and ready to apologize for their selfishness. Instead, she was confronted by Emily.

For an instant, she felt a twinge of guilt—and worry. Had Emily or Adriane realized she'd taken the unicorn horn?

No, that didn't appear to be it. Emily didn't look angry, just a little distracted.

Kara bent to collect what was left of the mass of papers she'd strewn about a few minutes ago. "Emily! Good. I—we have a lot of work to do."

"I can't do any concert stuff tonight," Emily said. "That's not why I'm here."

Kara slumped on the bed, tears threatening to spill once again. She wanted so much to tell Emily about the craziness with Lyra . . . but something told her to keep silent. She didn't understand it. The moment she opened her mouth to speak about the incident, her throat started closing with panic, her chest seizing up.

Emily sat beside her. "What's wrong, Kara?"

"Nothing. Just a weird day."

"Listen, I've been reading this book we found and—"

Kara was stunned. Did Emily know what she had been up to?

"We have to be really careful with this stuff." Emily dug into her bag. "Look, I photocopied part of the spellsinging book for you. I'll give Adriane another part and look through the rest myself." She handed some pages to Kara. "If this is what the Fairimental was talking about, then it's important. We need to read it and then combine our notes, figure out what to do with it."

"Why did they choose us?" Kara asked quietly.

"What do you mean?"

"Why did the Fairimentals have to choose us? They've ruined my life!" Kara wailed. "Everything was fine before I got involved with Ravenswood and this magic stuff!"

"Kara, I don't know why it's us . . . it just is." Emily said, softly. "Now it's up to us to decide what we're going to do about it."

"Like how? How far is this going to go?"

"I don't know," Emily said truthfully. "I think about that a lot, too. You remember what Adriane told us about the Prophecy of Three?"

"Yes." Kara remembered. The Fairimentals had told Adriane about the Prophecy in the Fairy Glen on Aldenmor.

One will follow her heart
One will see in darkness
One will change completely and utterly

"Adriane followed her heart when she went after Storm on Aldenmor. I saw in darkness when I led us across the magic web and back home to Ravenswood . . ."

"So . . . the third one is mine," Kara said, eyes opening wide. "One will change completely . . . but I don't want to change!"

Emily took Kara's hand. "My dad always says life is change. I think he means that we're going to change no matter what we do, if we want to or not."

Kara flashed on the magnificent white unicorn that had taken her to the beaches of Avalon. Fairy wraiths, the guardians of Avalon, had asked her if she was ready to become the blazing star.

"Close your eyes, child," the wraith told her.

Kara closed her eyes. A soft breeze dried her tears.

"Now open them."

Kara blinked and looked out at the gleaming ocean. The strange glowing mist still hid whatever lay underneath.

"Do you see any difference?"

"No," Kara said, confused.

The wraith sighed, a sound like the wind crying.

"Only those who truly understand the magic can find Avalon."

"Where is Avalon? How do we get there?"

"There are fairy maps to guide the blazing star."

Only the blazing star could open the fairy map to Avalon—the one she had lost.

Kara blinked and looked back at her friend's warm smile.

"Emily, something *is* happening to me," Kara admitted. "How do I know what to do? What's right?"

The healer smiled. "When I see Ozzie, or Ariel, or Storm, or any of the other animals, and the way they look at me, they way they love me and you and Adriane . . . I just know it's the right thing to help them. Because we're friends and we love them."

"Yeah . . ." Kara agreed.

"That's one thing that will never change."

Kara sighed and walked to the window, looking for a pair of golden wings. "I wish I could believe that."

"Your magic is different than the rest of ours," Emily continued. "It's special. We all know that. But only you can choose how to change. And we'll stick by you no matter what happens." Emily smiled.

Kara gave her a quick smile in return. "I'd better not change into a flobbin!"

The two friends laughed.

"I have to go," Emily said. "But look over the spells and we'll meet tomorrow at the glade to talk about what we do next. Okay?"

"Okay."

Emily gave Kara a hug, then left.

Kara smiled. She was lucky to have Emily as a friend. Suddenly the locket around Kara's neck glowed and her mind began to drift. Kara knew she should have come clean about the unicorn horn, but she still needed it. She looked over the pages Emily had copied for her. There were spells and lessons on how to use singing to control magic. Here's an interesting one: "Spell of Silence"—I'd like to use that on Adriane, Kara mused.

Then she thought about the power she had unleashed behind the school. If her one little rhyme had been so powerful, especially when combined with the unicorn horn, maybe these real spells could help her make the finals.

She wished she could get her hands on the book itself, but this would have to do.

Kara clutched the locket close to her heart.

She was changing, all right. And it looked like everything was going to turn her way after all.

10

*K*ARA STOOD BACKSTAGE at the school auditorium, nervously twirling a lock of long, blond hair. After running through a half dozen outfits, Kara settled on a hot pink pullover, brown suede pants, and her new Valero boots. One moment she thought the outfit looked stylish beyond compare—and the next, she was convinced it was hideous. She hadn't been truly satisfied with anything she'd tried on. Nothing would be good enough, Kara was beginning to think . . . especially herself.

Even more frustrating, she had gone through every page of the spellsinging book Emily had copied for her and hadn't been able to find a single rhyme that could make her magically enhanced singing voice last. The spells all seemed to have been created for some other purpose. She had tried to sing as soon as she had gotten up and discovered that her voice was back to normal— horrible! But not for long. She pulled her shirt down over the unicorn horn concealed in her back pocket.

Kara stole a quick peek at the audience. Inky, who was presiding over this round of the competition, was chitchatting with reporters. Johnny was talking with folks in the front row, mostly members of the Town Council and their families, along with teachers and a few representatives of the school board. Web cam operators had set up their equipment to capture the entire event.

Johnny suddenly turned and looked right at Kara. The instant their gazes met, she felt the locket tingle and her fear melted away, replaced by excitement. A barrage of flashes illuminated Kara against the curtain as half a dozen photographers swung their cameras into action. She produced her perfect Kara smile for the crowd.

Touching the locket, she felt more determined than ever to be a winner and make him proud.

A group of girls gathered around Kara.

"That is so cool, Johnny gave you his locket!" a girl from her homeroom said.

"Can I see it?"

Some were just excited, and wanted to touch it, or try it on—not that Kara would let them. Several others really were jealous and shot daggers at her for wearing the locket at all.

Good, Kara thought. Maybe some of them would get psyched out, that would make it easier for her.

Closing her eyes and leaning against a back wall, Kara smiled.

A loud knock made Kara open her eyes. She was startled to see Adriane standing before her wearing a black vest, stylish jeans, and black leather boots. Her hair, glistening with subtle red highlights, looked amazing.

"Hey," Adriane said.

Kara nodded. "You look . . . good."

"Thanks, I just, um . . ." Adriane frowned. "We need to talk."

Kara hesitated, a sudden pang of guilt jabbing her . . . then she shrugged. "Now?"

"It's just . . . some strange things have been going on."

"You *would* think that," Kara muttered.

Adriane's eyes widened and she looked ready to deliver a nasty comeback—then she forced a smile into place. "Look, I haven't been myself lately. I don't know why it became so important to win this contest."

Kara tapped her foot, waiting.

"Okay, what do *you* think is going on?" Adriane asked.

"Nothing," Kara said impatiently, looking past Adriane to where the contestants were starting to line up.

Kara had drawn her lot when she first arrived. She was

number twenty-three. Thank goodness she didn't have to go first!

"Can't this wait till later? They're almost ready," she said.

"No, it can't," Adriane stated. "Listen, Kara, I know you've been really . . . busy lately."

"So?"

"*So,* we all need to work together if we're going to figure this out," Adriane insisted.

Kara restrained her urge to agree with Adriane. She wanted to trust her friend . . . but some instinct told her not to let her guard down.

"I don't know why I pushed you," Adriane said, "I don't want to compete with you . . . I mean, let's just call a truce before—"

Kara stared at Adriane cautiously. "Before what?"

"Well . . . before something else happens," Adriane whispered, adding, "You know it and I know it. I've heard you sing, you know."

Anger flared within Kara. "And you're worried I'm gonna embarrass myself?"

"What?" Adriane threw her hands up. "This contest . . . it was *never* supposed to be about the *two of us.* This is for Ravenswood. You're the president, our leader. If you go out there and—"

"That's it," Kara said, her cheeks flushing crimson. She pushed past Adriane to join the others.

"I didn't mean it like that!" Adriane called.

Kara stopped listening. She took her place in line and saw both Adriane and Heather take their places close to the front. Good. She didn't want to deal with either of them right now. She was nervous enough as it was—and Adriane trying to psych her out . . . That was really too much to deal with.

As the music started and the curtain went up, Kara noticed two of the other girls casting worried looks at her locket. Suddenly feeling like a prize creep, Kara slipped the locket under her blouse, hiding it from view. A minute ago, she thought it was so cool showing it off. What was happening to her?

Then the show kicked off!

The waiting—and the watching—turned out to be a lot harder than Kara had expected. One by one, boys and girls took the stage, and some were *really* good. Much better than Kara . . . and she knew it.

"And now, contestant number six, the rock and roll warrior!" Inky announced.

Adriane leaped into the spotlight, jamming on her cherry red Fender guitar. She swung the guitar back over her shoulder and sung a classic rock song. She was extraordinary! Kara twiddled with the locket again, feeling its energy course through her. Then Inky was onstage again, introducing "lucky" number seven— Heather Wilson. The redhead started to sing and the entire auditorium fell silent. Everyone backstage was buzzing—even Adriane—saying Heather not only had it in the bag to be one of the finalists, but that she would be the one to beat on Saturday during the preshow! Kara noticed several of the girls who were scheduled to go on after Heather walk away from the line and bow out. Others were asking to have their numbers reassigned. It seemed no one wanted to face the humiliation of following Heather's amazing performance. Kara saw Inky nodding and smiling, hanging on her every note. Even Johnny was enthusiastically caught up in the performance.

Kara knew she should support her friend, but she just couldn't bring herself to care. Instead, she drew comfort from the warmth of Johnny's locket. It began to pulse with light in her fingers—

"Kara! You're up next!" One of the teachers rushed over to her.

Kara allowed the teacher to lead her to her place in front of the handful of remaining contestants. She nervously rubbed the locket around her neck. Several of the other girls looked at it once again—and she thought about putting it away.

Then she saw Johnny sitting in the first row, front and center, staring right at her with his bright, winning smile. His eyes flashed with blue fire.

No, she thought. Why should I hide it? This is my lucky charm!

Kara was ushered onstage. The bright lights seared her eyes as she heard the music start up. It was one of

Johnny's hits, a song she knew by heart. And so far she had been the only one to pick this song.

Two points for me, she thought, terrified. She looked out into the audience and felt her head go light, her knees threaten to turn to water. Just about everyone she knew was watching her, waiting for her to mess up . . .

Well, to heck with that! Kara thought. Raising her head defiantly, she took the microphone. She looked at Johnny and saw his lips moving, as if he were singing the first verse himself.

And then—

The world stopped. For just a moment Kara experienced a sudden silence, a vacuum that drew all light and sound and sensation from her. She thought she was passing out.

No, this can't be happening!

She reached for the power of the unicorns and felt a sparkle of fire where the locket hung.

With a twirl, Kara stepped into a choreographed dance move, moving in sync with the beat. Her voice sang out, filling the auditorium and carrying the melody in perfect pitch. Rocking out, Kara danced up a storm as the crowd was swept to their feet with the excitement of her performance.

She was being showered with applause. Kara shuddered, feeling disoriented.

"You rocked, girl! Totally cool," Inky said, taking the microphone from her. "Kara Davies, everyone!" He called out. "Everyone, give it up for contestant number twenty-three, Kara Davies!"

The applause rose and Kara bowed, basking in the adoration of the crowd. She could certainly get used to this.

Just before she left the stage, she saw Johnny wink at her.

Backstage, Adriane glared at her suspiciously, but Kara didn't care.

The next hour passed in a blur. The other girls did their numbers, with Inky off in the corner making notes about them. Then he took the stage and announced the finalists.

Heather had made the cut, *duh* there. But so had two girls Kara barely knew, along with Adriane, and—

"Our fifth finalist, Kara Davies!" Inky roared.

Kara raced out onto the stage, thrilled to be part of the winner's circle. She posed with the others for photographs.

"We'll see you all tomorrow." Inky waved. "It's going to be a great day for Ravenswood!"

Kara was ecstatic—for all of about five seconds.

Before she could say a word, Adriane grabbed her arm and yanked her aside.

"Okay," the tall girl said. "I don't know how you did it, and I don't care."

"Did . . . did what?" Kara asked.

"You went out there and you didn't stink," Adriane said bluntly.

"Yeah, thanks," Kara said. "I had so much encouragement from my *friends*." She delivered that last word like an icy dagger.

"And some help, too, no doubt!"

"What do you mean?" Kara asked, innocently.

"I mean—this!" Adriane held up her wrist. The wolf stone was pulsing with strong amber light. "I know you used some kind of magic! Don't deny it!"

"No way." Kara's eyes darted back and forth, trying to see if anyone was close enough to hear them.

"You cheated!" Adriane hissed.

"My singing is just as good as yours," Kara countered.

"In your dreams. You're bowing out of the finals!"

Kara stared at Adriane in absolute fury. "You've got to be kidding!"

One look into Adriane's eyes and Kara knew she was deadly serious.

"I *have* to be in the finals!"

"Why, Kara? Just what is so important about singing on that stage?"

Kara stopped short. When she actually thought about it, she had no logical reason.

"This is about Ravenswood!" Adriane continued. "The spotlight needs to be on the preserve, the animals, what we're trying to do for them . . . not on you."

"So why aren't you backing out?" Kara asked. "You

cheated, too! You used magic to get the home court advantage. You've got Johnny living right next door. You think people aren't going to talk about that if you win?"

"I haven't been getting Johnny's attention every single minute. You have. I mean . . . look at what you're wearing!"

Shaking with rage, Kara clutched the locket.

"Fine! But if I can't sing in the contest, neither can you!" Kara said to Adriane's face. "Or I'll tell everyone how you practiced with Johnny at Ravenswood!"

Adriane looked furious.

"Do we have a deal?" Kara asked.

"Fine! I don't want to be in this stupid contest anymore!" And she stormed off.

Kara turned her back on Adriane and went to talk with Inky. He wasn't exactly happy to hear that she was withdrawing, but there were backup choices for the contest. As long as this is what Kara really wanted . . . well, then he'd be fine with it.

So maybe she wouldn't sing with Johnny as the contest winner, Kara thought.

There were plenty of other ways to get even for what Adriane had pulled. She looked in her backpack at the photocopies.

Plenty of other spells, too.

11

*K*ARA DIDN'T SLEEP at all that night. Now it was morning—*the* morning, the concert was *today*—but she couldn't get out of bed. She lay buried under blankets and pillows.

The song had gone so well. Kara would never forget how it felt to stand in front of all those people, to be under the glaring lights, to hear their applause. But she had taken a magical shortcut, leaping right over the part that was really difficult, heading right to the instant reward she had craved.

Which . . . wasn't bad, right? She really had delivered on that song, and if things had gone the way they should have, the way they were meant to, she would have netted that spot singing with Johnny. Only—Adriane had discovered her secret, part of it anyway. That she'd used magic to cheat her way to winning.

Kara was furious with Adriane, yet she also felt relieved. She hated lying and she hated being a cheater! What had possessed her to even consider such a stupid thing? What would her parents and friends think of her if they knew? She chewed her lip. And the way she had treated Heather . . . that was so cruel. To top it off, she had even destroyed school property! No wonder she hadn't slept much.

She tossed the pillows, kicked away the blankets, and sprang out of bed. She would meet Adriane and Emily at the portal field and use the dragonfly phone to contact Zach. Then she would spill it all and beg her friends to forgive her. She would return the horn immediately before something really terrible happened. She would forget singing onstage with Johnny and get back to what was really important: getting the word out to the world about Ravenswood!

Someone knocked at her door. "Hey, sleeping beauty!" her father called. "You've got a visitor!"

"I'm not here!" Kara replied. A visitor. Probably Molly or Tiffany . . .

"Not here?" came another voice, light and musical, from downstairs. "Not even for me?"

It was Johnny!

Flying into a pile of clothes, she threw on a pair of jeans and a T-shirt. She yanked open the door, barreled past her startled father, bolted down the steps—then stopped short.

Johnny was standing in her living room. Wavy black hair brushed his forehead. His gorgeous blue eyes twinkled.

Mayor Davies cleared his throat. "How about some breakfast, Johnny?"

"No thanks, Mayor D," Johnny said. "Just stopped by with a quick update for the Ravenswood president."

"Well, thanks again for coming to Stonehill—we all really appreciate your generosity," Kara's dad said, walking back to the kitchen. "Good luck with the show."

"The pleasure is all mine," Johnny said to the mayor, but his smile was for Kara. "Ready for the big day?"

Kara nervously ran her hand through her hair, which she knew was a total mess. "Um, uh . . . sure," she said, accompanied by a self-conscious little laugh.

"I have a feeling this is going to be a day people will talk about for years to come." His melodic tones filled her with visions of rock and roll glory.

Kara smiled back. Cool.

"So, what's up?" she asked.

"Inky tells me you've decided to back out of the competition."

"Uh, yeah . . ." How was she going to explain this one?

"That's just like you, you know," Johnny said, moving past her to examine the family photos on the fireplace mantle. "Always thinking of your friends first."

"Uh . . . I guess . . ."

"You figured it was a conflict," he reasoned. "With you being the president of Ravenswood and all, right?"

"It's not that I didn't want to sing with you . . ."

"Did you?"

"Oh, yes, more than anything!" Kara wasn't lying about that.

"Good. Because I have something for you."

Kara waited. The locket suddenly became warm. Her skin tingled and she tried to stay cool—but suddenly it was hard to think straight.

"I wrote a song for you," Johnny said.

Kara practically stopped breathing. "You what?"

Johnny took a sheet of paper from his pocket. "I wrote it originally for Be*Tween. You know, Inky manages them too. We're pretty sure it's going to be a number one hit. The problem is—Be*Tween's missing. The way I heard it, they wanted a little time off."

Kara's heart thundered as she scanned the lyrics. He had to be kidding . . . but the look in his eyes was icy calm, deadly serious. This wasn't a gag.

"It's called 'Shine Your Light,'" Johnny explained. "It's about finding the path that's right for you—letting friends know who you really are inside."

"That's crazy!" Kara squealed.

"It's the least I can do for all the work you've done organizing the concert. And like I said before, you've got something . . . special."

Then she felt the heat of Johnny's locket . . . and thought of the unicorn horn. Such amazing magic, all for her.

"And I want you to sing the song tonight, for the first time, during the concert," Johnny said.

"Wow!" A brand-new Johnny Conrad song, and Kara was going to debut it tonight! "But what about the contest?"

"Don't worry about that," Johnny answered her. "We'll get that over with early on. You're going to be the show-stopper!"

Kara just couldn't believe it.

"I'll let you in on a secret. You know what being a star is?"

"What?" she whispered.

"When you shine brighter than anyone else in the world."

Kara smiled, eyes wide.

"Brief, bright . . . and then it's over."

"Not for you, Johnny," Kara said, holding her breath.

"Oh, yes, even for me. I'm just this month's musical flavor. A year from now no one will have ever heard of Johnny Conrad. I'll be yesterday's news."

"No *way!*"

He shrugged. "There will be someone newer, cooler. It's just the way it is. But while we *are* stars, we do our best to shine, shooting across the heavens in a blaze of glory! You get all you can, any way you can! And tonight your light will shine brighter than anyone else's!"

Kara was speechless. Is this what it meant to be the blazing star? To flame brighter than anything else—only to burn out in a blaze of glory? She shuddered.

12

"*B*LAZE!"

"Barney!"

"Fiona!"

"Fred!"

"Goldie!"

Adriane, Emily, Balthazar, Ozzie, Storm, Ronif, and Rasha moved through the portal field calling the names of Kara's dragonflies. Although usually complete pests, the magical mini-dragons were useful at times. They had woven the dreamcatcher from strands of the magic web to protect the portal. They could also open a small window to Aldenmor.

But without Kara the dragonflies were not showing up.

"One thing I can say about her," Adriane grumbled. "She's consistent."

The early morning mist had evaporated, revealing the deep woods of the preserve that surrounded the field.

Emily looked at her watch again. Nine o'clock. Kara was an hour late.

"All right," she said. "We need another plan."

"It's useless," Ozzie complained. "Those dragonflies will only come to Kara!"

Adriane turned to Storm. "Storm, do you think you can reach out and call to Moonshadow?"

"*The wolfsong is strong, but not strong enough on its own to cross between worlds.*"

Emily's face brightened. "This dreamcatcher is made of the magic web itself." She turned to Storm. "It might amplify your call."

"*The wolves did contact me through the portal once before,*" Storm said.

"But how do we open the portal?" Balthazar asked.

"Lorelei's horn can open it," Adriane said.

"How about with this?" Emily asked, looking through the pages from the spellsinging book she had taken from her backpack. She handed pages to Adriane and some to Ozzie.

"I saw Summoning Spells in here the other night," she said. "Try to find them. Maybe we can use one to summon the portal."

"All right," Adriane said, looking through the pages. "Beats standing around waiting for Goldilocks." Considering the way Kara had been acting lately, the last thing Adriane wanted to admit was that they actually needed her.

"Here's one," Ozzie exclaimed. "*Say it loud but reverse the words, you'll speak in tongues from a mirror's curve.*"

"That's a backward spell, Ozzie," Emily said. "Makes everything you say come out backward."

"haG! I have enough trouble just being a ferret!"

"*Float like a cloud, so high, so light,*" Adriane read, "*Hear these words and fly like a kite.*"

"Lightness of Being Spell," Emily said. "Makes you lighter than air."

"Can't wait to try *that* one out on Rapunzel," Adriane giggled.

Emily gave her a stern look.

"You're right," Adriane commented. "She'd just put designer cement in her boots."

"Here." Emily found the page she had been looking for and scanned the text.

> *Hear our call, strong and clear*
> *We use this song to bring you near*
> *We summon the image we see inside*
> *We need your power, by this spell, abide*

"Sound okay to you?" Adriane asked the others.

"If we all focus on the dreamcatcher, it might work," Balthazar said.

"Just one last thing," Emily said. "These spell songs can only be used *once*. After we use it, we'll forget how it goes. The words will disappear from the book, and probably from these pages, too. I read that in the introduction."

"Okay, so we get one shot. Let's add some healing and wolf power to the mix," Adriane said, holding up her wrist and exposing her wolf stone.

Emily held her rainbow jewel next to Adriane's jewel. A spark of magic jumped between the stones, connecting them.

"You take it, Adriane." Emily handed the page to her friend.

Adriane started humming a small phrase from a familiar song and then added the lyrics of the spell.

> *Hear our call, strong and clear.*
> *We use this song to bring you near.*
> *We summon the portal to see inside.*
> *With our magic, by this spell, abide.*

At first, nothing happened. The wind stirred a little then died down. Adriane had reached the end of the song, but the words were still fresh in her mind, the characters still printed on the pages.

"Once more," Emily said to Adriane. She turned to the others. "Picture the portal in your mind. Focus."

Adriane nodded and sang again, and this time—the air began to swirl faster. Winds blew across the grass. Adriane looked down—the words were vanishing from the page. They had done it right!

The air filled with twinkling lights as a giant shape took form in front of them. With a *whoosh* of air, the portal opened. And the dreamcatcher sparkled before it, hanging in the sky. The intricate weaving of threads caught the light of the morning sun and glistened like a thousand diamonds.

"We did it!" Ronif yelled.

"Hurry, Storm," Emily said. "I don't know how long the spell will last."

The silver wolf stood in front of the dreamcatcher and raised her silver-maned head majestically. She howled into the swirling portal. In response, the dreamcatcher gently fluttered.

Then Adriane threw back her head and howled with her friend.

Mist filled the circle in the center of the dreamcatcher.

"Again!" Adriane called out. Storm howled the wolf song, a song filled with thousands of years of wolf memories, connecting her to the pack.

Suddenly, another howl cut through the morning air, echoing across the field.

"*Moonshadow!*" Storm called out. "*Hear me!*"

The group gathered and peered into the dream-catcher's center.

The mist began to clear and they saw darkness. Dimly, moonlight shone over tree-covered hills spreading into the distance. Dark shapes moved.

"*Moonshadow,*" Storm called out again.

A giant black wolf head slid into the misty picture, bright golden eyes aglow. "*Stormbringer! My heart fills with happiness!*"

"*As does mine, pack leader,*" Storm answered.

"*There is so- rarrg!*" A blond head of hair shoved the big wolf aside. Zach's face filled the window.

"Adriane! Are you there, too?" Zach called out.

"Zach! It's me!" Adriane's heart filled with joy at the sight of her friend. "Are you all right?"

"Yes. We've left the Packhom*garhh*—" Zach was nudged out of the window by the black wolf.

"*There is much to say and not much time,*" Moonshadow warned.

"Tell us," Emily called.

"*The Black Fire has stopped raining from the skies.*"

"That's good news!" Adriane exclaimed.

Zach shoved in next to his wolf brother, angling for position. "We thought so, at first. We've been camped on the foothills near the Shadowlands, sending in scouting teams."

He looks tired, Adriane thought. She wished she could

sit beside him, talk and laugh with him like she had done on Aldenmor. She tried to ignore the sadness welling in her chest. "What is the Dark Sorceress up to now?" she asked.

"She's planning something big!" Zach told them. "She built four giant crystals. We think they've been designed to hold magic, lots of it."

"*Aldenmor grows barren of magic. We fear for the Fairimentals!*" Moonshadow howled sadly. Howls of the pack echoed behind him.

"If there is so little magic left on Aldenmor, then why has she built these crystals?" Balthazar asked.

"She means to draw magic from somewhere else," Zach said worriedly.

No one had to ask where that might be. There was only one place that held the kind of magic the sorceress desired. The home of all magic: Avalon.

Zach was silent for a few seconds. "She has the fairy map with the correct sequence of portals to Avalon."

"*I, too, carry a fairy map of Aldenmor, given to me by my human wolf sister!*" Moonshadow managed to stick his nose in.

Adriane smiled. "It was a gift from the Fairimentals. I just brought it to you."

"Wait!" Emily said. "You can only use fairy magic if it's given to you. The sorceress stole that fairy map. She can't use it."

"But there is one person it *was* meant for," Ozzie said, almost to himself. "Who *can* use it."

"Kara," Emily and Adriane said at the same time.

"The portal is closing," Ronif yelled.

"The Fairimentals were trying to tell us something about the fairy map," Adriane said.

"Be careful." Zach said, talking faster. "The sorceress may have sent someone to your world to get Kara to open it for her."

"But nothing bad can come through the dream-catcher," Ronif pointed out.

"Someone new *did* show up at Ravenswood recently . . ." Emily began.

"Yeah, someone who *volunteered* to come," Adriane continued.

"Someone who Kara is spending an awful lot of time with . . ." Emily added.

"Johnny!" Adriane finished.

"Adriane, whatever happens," Zach called out," you can't let Kara open that fairy map!"

Adriane nodded. "Stay strong, Zach. I promise we will see you and the pack again. Soon! And you'd better be right at the portal when I get there!" She had to fight back her tears.

Zach smiled, his green eyes warm and full of light as he faded away.

The portal was vanishing, swirling sparkling lights twinkling back into mist.

Suddenly, a mighty howl rose from the entire wolf pack, reaching across the worlds. Adriane and Storm howled back, cementing their bond with the ancient wolf song, and the spirit of Avalon.

"Adriane!"

Gran was standing in the open doorway of their cottage, waving. "Come here a moment."

"Can it wait?" Adriane asked, pausing on the cobblestone pathway behind Ravenswood Manor. "I'm kind of in a hurry."

"This will just take a minute. I need to show you something."

Shrugging, Adriane turned and followed her grandmother into the house.

"What's up?" she asked as they entered the living room.

"I don't feel so good," Gran told her, pointing at the couch.

Adriane spun around—and was shocked to see . . . her *grandmother* lying on it? She heard the front door lock behind her.

"Huh?" Adriane whirled around to face the other grandmother, who was smiling sweetly. There were *two* Grans. But that was impossible!

"This is where you're supposed to say: 'My, what sharp teeth you have, grandmother.'" The imposter leaned toward her with a little snicker.

Before Adriane could react, the old woman sprang at her with a strength and speed that Adriane would have thought impossible—if she'd had the chance to think at all. She was too busy screaming as her grandmother's face changed. For a brief moment, Adriane thought she was looking at Johnny; then the creature's skin turned green and scaly, fingernails turned to talons, teeth grew sharp and long, and the eyes blazed with a terrible inhuman fire.

"Time for a little nap, dear," the Skultum said, its huge hands covering Adriane's face.

Adriane tried to raise her stone but the dark magic sunk deep, paralyzing her senses. She caught a sudden, terrifying glimpse of the creature's form changing once more, becoming a perfect duplicate of Adriane herself. Then all was black.

13

*R*OWS OF PEOPLE, in line for the concert, stretched all the way down the driveway leading into Ravenswood Preserve. Behind the manor, families strolled with children in the crisp afternoon sun; teens hung out by the huge speakers blasting music from the stage set on the great lawn. The entire town had shown up. Kara had heard that over three thousand people were in attendance, not huge by stadium standards, but a smashing success for Stonehill and for Ravenswood. Concession stands were doing brisk business selling popcorn, hot dogs, and juice. Everyone wore Ravenswood T-shirts, sweatshirts, hats, and bandanas. There were even small stuffed toys of favorite Ravenswood animals: Ariel, Storm, Lyra, and Ozzie.

A huge banner hung behind the stage. The words

SAVE RAVENSWOOD! were stenciled over an image of a giant dreamcatcher. That had been Adriane's idea.

Kara wandered, waving to the crowds spread out across the great lawn. This was going unbelievably well, she thought. She looked great in her new rhinestone accented jeans, boots, and brand-new faux-fur trimmed jacket over her Ravenswood tee. So why did she feel like a total loser? She knew exactly why. Although she had learned Johnny's new song, she was torn between using the magical help of the unicorn horn and just being herself, no matter what she sounded like. The pressure of debuting a Johnny Conrad original was unbearable! She had never felt so nervous, so out of sorts. How could she *not* use the magic!

"Kara!"

It was her dad. Mayor Davies was standing with the Town Council near the side of the stage, being interviewed by a group of reporters. The mayor was waving to her. "Kara, honey! Over here!"

Kara trudged over as a woman reporter stuck the mike in her face. "What's your message to the world about Ravenswood?"

Kara thought hard. All those long months of planning, all the worry, the problems, the dreams, had all come down to these few moments. Images of her friends flashed through her mind: Emily, Adriane, Molly, Heather, Tiffany . . . the animals, Ozzie, Storm, and, once upon a time—Lyra.

"Ravenswood is more than just a wildlife preserve,"

she said at last. "It's . . . It represents our whole planet. We share our world with animals who count on us, and we count on them. And with help from all our friends, we can make our world a better place for everyone."

"Well said." The reporter was clearly impressed. "I'm putting this on the national feed," she told an elated council. "Ravenswood is an inspiration for all of us."

The reporter shook Kara's hand. "The whole world will soon see what a fine example you have set for young people everywhere."

Kara stiffened. What if the whole world saw that she was a cheater? "Um, thank you," she said uncomfortably. She had to get out of here—and take care of this once and for all. "Dad, I have to go . . . check on some final details."

"Okay, honey." The mayor didn't miss a beat, continuing to smile and talk proudly about Stonehill's future as Kara slipped away.

A fine example for young people everywhere . . . What a crock! She *had* to fix this. Clutching her backpack tight against her chest, she hurried through the happy crowds and snuck in through the back door of the manor.

She scurried up the stairs to the library, determined to do what was right—put the unicorn horn back. Whatever happened onstage later would happen. At least she would do it on her own. She was through with the cheating, the lying. In the end, she knew she had only deceived herself.

She reached the library door and was surprised to find

it unlocked and open a crack. Then she heard sounds from within. *Click-clack. Tap-tap-tap.*

Someone was using the computer!

Kara grabbed the knob and swung the door open, ready to ask Emily or Adriane why the door was unlocked with so many strangers on the grounds.

But it wasn't Emily or Adriane at the computer. It was Johnny.

Johnny Conrad sat at the keyboard to their secret computer, weird images flickering on the screen before him. He looked over at Kara and grinned. "Hey, what's up?"

"I—I—" she stammered. Trying to mask her surprise, she ran her hands through her mane of blond hair. "What are *you* doing in here?"

The computer was way off-limits to anyone but the girls. The files held all kinds of secrets about . . . magic.

Johnny looked confused. "I was just checking my e-mail. Adriane told me it would be okay. What, did I do something wrong?"

Worried that someone else might walk in, Kara swung the door closed behind her. Johnny seemed relaxed and confident as ever, not at all like someone who was about to perform in front of thousands of people . . . in about ten minutes! "Aren't you supposed to be, like, in your dressing room, getting ready?"

"I don't have a dressing room. This isn't exactly the Staples Center, you know," he joked. "Hey. Check this out. There's a live web feed of the whole event."

Kara walked over and stared at the screen. A window was open. It displayed a live camera view of the stage and great lawns. Had Johnny seen her walking to the manor?

"Adriane also showed me all these cool files you've set up for your Web site." Johnny swung back around and hit some keys. Pictures of the animals appeared in windows. "It's really great."

Kara drew a sharp breath. Crossing her arms over her chest, Kara cautiously came closer and got a better look at the screen. Had Adriane completely lost her mind? The girls had made a solemn pact to keep the computer secret!

"So, you all set for your number?" Johnny got up and stretched like a sleek jungle cat. He moved to one of the large windows overlooking the event out back. The window was open and the sound of laughter drifted up to the library.

"I guess." Kara frowned as she joined him. They looked out at the vast crowd. Onstage, techies were finishing the last of the sound and light checks. "So . . . Adriane let you in here?" she asked.

"Well, *yeah*." Johnny smiled. Then his gaze narrowed. "What—did you think I picked the lock or something? If I wanted to be sneaky I would have snuck in at, like, three in the morning."

Good point, Kara realized. Yet . . .

"I just don't get why Adriane would do that," Kara said suspiciously. "Some of the things we keep in here are . . . private."

For the first time, Johnny looked uncomfortable. "You and Adriane *are* friends, right?"

"Of course. Why do you ask that?"

Johnny pointed out the open window. Chants and cheers began to rise from the happy crowd. "Johnny! Johnny!"

"Remember what we talked about, about what being a star means?" Johnny asked her.

"Yes." Kara felt the locket grow warm against her skin.

"Stars have to make sacrifices. Look at the crowd out there. When you're onstage, it's all for them. "

Kara felt the excitement of performing starting to build.

"They expect the best you can be," Johnny reminded her, "and you have to deliver, no matter what it takes. Being one in a million means standing alone. It changes everything. People you thought were friends can turn on you, betray you."

The words snaked into Kara's mind. *Adriane has always been jealous of me.*

Johnny looked at her with his dark, soulful blue eyes. "How well do you really know Adriane?"

Kara was taken aback. Had he read her mind? "I've only known her for a few months . . . Why?"

"When you're a star, friends can do things, act weird. Has anything happened recently? Anything that, I dunno, might have *changed* her?"

The locket sparkled, tingling against her skin—and

suddenly, Kara thought about the time Adriane had spent on Aldenmor . . . and in the Dark Sorceress's dungeon. Was it possible that Adriane had come back *changed* somehow? That maybe the Dark Sorceress had gotten to her, had made her evil? It would sure explain why Adriane had been acting like such a little *witch* lately.

"Adriane . . . went away for a little while," Kara said. "She met some not-so-nice people."

"I've seen it before." Johnny rubbed his temples. "Listen, I hate to be the one to tell you this, but it's for your own good."

"What? Tell me," Kara demanded.

"Your friend Adriane has been asking me and Inky, right from the beginning, how she can get a record contract. She wants to sing her own song, which Inky thinks could be a single, onstage at the concert."

Kara flinched. The locket was even warmer now—but nowhere near as fiery as her anger. "What else?"

"She said . . . *she* should be the blazing star. Not you."

Kara was speechless.

Johnny nodded. "Does that mean anything to you? Was that, like, supposed to be a name you wanted to record under?"

"I . . . I don't believe that," Kara stammered.

Johnny's eyes filled with sympathy. "Well, she's in the ballroom right now, rehearsing."

Her brow furrowed in confusion and anger. She spun around and started pacing. "I cannot believe that girl!"

Kara yelled. "She told me she wasn't going to sing onstage. We had a deal!"

Johnny watched her. "I'm sorry. But like I said, when you're a star, friends can turn on you."

The locket flared—Kara was enraged. How could Adriane do this to her?

Spellsinging under his breath so softly she wouldn't hear it, wouldn't detect his lips moving at all, he exerted just enough influence. He had to be careful, the talisman could focus her blazing star magic, but it was no match for the magic of the unicorns.

"Why did you come to the library, Kara?"

"Huh? I was going to return something . . ."

"Remember what I said. You need to use whatever you can to show the world that *you* are the blazing star. That's the only way you can beat Adriane." A slight smile played across Johnny's lips.

"Oh, don't worry about that. I am going to blaze so bright the entire audience will need sunglasses!" She didn't give another thought to returning the unicorn horn or leaving Johnny alone in the library. Kara stormed out of the room.

The *only* thing she cared about right now was dealing with Adriane once and for all!

Johnny Conrad watched her go. A cruel smile appeared on his perfect face.

He hummed the first few notes of "Shine Your Light" and spread his fingers. A twinkling ball of stars winked into existence, floating in midair. He grinned as he stared at the sparkling fairy map, bright silver stars in its center, waiting to shine . . . so much like a *blazing star*.

He was, of course, much more powerful than Kara as a spellsinger, but magic was more than spellsinging . . . much more.

"Poor, confused little Kara," Johnny sneered, raising his hand and touching the floating orb.

The little fool. He knew her weaknesses, her vulnerabilities . . . She was so pathetically easy to read—and to manipulate. Completely ruled by emotions and with no gem of her own. Getting her to use the unicorn horn had been easy, although he had been surprised how powerful the magic was in her hands. But even that had proved a blessing in disguise. He chuckled at his selection of words.

With her power—strengthened by her use of the unicorn horn—his spellsong could not fail. Kara would spellsing the words that would unlock the fairy map. The portals between this world, Aldenmor, and Avalon itself would open in just the right order, laying the path for the sorceress to do as she pleased.

He had to make *very sure* that Kara sang her song tonight. The locket could help to sway her, influence her, but it could not control her completely.

There was one final thing left to do: to make her use her magic with enough force to trigger the map. She had to let her fire rage—and turn completely against her friends.

He smiled, his voice musical, chiming and tremulous. Before him, the fairy map returned to its invisible hiding place. "Places to go, people to be . . ."

Closing his eyes, he stood by the open window. He concentrated, reaching out with his otherworldly senses.

"Show time," Johnny said. Throwing his arms open wide, he allowed his form to shimmer and change, to melt as his arms transformed to wings. His body morphed into a large, dark bat.

With a flutter of wings, the Skultum flew out the window.

14

THROWING OPEN THE double doors, Kara stomped into the large ballroom. The clip-clop of her boots against the hardwood floors echoed in the empty space. All of the band's equipment had been moved out. The formal dining table, which had been moved to the side, was covered with bottles of water, fresh fruit in large bowls, and platters with sandwiches, cakes, and other leftover sweet treats. Drapes covered the immense windows, leaving the room dark.

Kara stopped and stared in utter amazement as she saw what hung on the walls. The heavy wood-framed pictures of wilderness scenes were gone. In their place were posters, each featuring Adriane singing, dancing, and playing guitar. They read: #1 HOT HOT HOTTIE, THE NEW MUSIC SENSATION, OOPS, I WIN AGAIN!

Kara was stunned.

Suddenly, a spotlight splashed onto the wood floor at one end of the room. From the dark shadows, Adriane stepped into the center of it. She was decked out in shiny silver pants, black crop top emblazoned with the words ROCK 'N ROLL WARRIOR, silver boots, and sunglasses. Her hair was layered in streaks of red, gold, and pink. She had a sparkling purple metal-flake guitar strapped across her back. With a swift martial arts move, she swung the guitar in position and strummed a loud chord.

The chord filled the room, resonating with power. Kara stood in total shock as Adriane began to sing.

> *One, two—take a look at you*
> *You're standing there, you think I care*
> *But don't you know*
> *Anything you can do*
> *I can do better*

The spotlight followed Adriane as she moved around the room, singing and dancing like a superstar.

> *Three, four—you're such a bore*
> *It's all about me, can't you see*
> *That in the end*

Anything you can do
I can do better

"That's enough!" Kara yelled in fury.

Adriane strummed the guitar one more time, then swung it back over her shoulder. "And that's just my warm up number," she said coolly.

"You look totally . . . *stupid!*" Kara announced.

Adriane laughed. "You're funny."

Kara crossed her arms. "We had a deal! You said you weren't going to sing in the show," she yelled.

"I said I wasn't going to sing in the contest! You're the one sneaking around getting your own spot! Why shouldn't I get *my* own spot? I'm so much better than you'll ever be!" Adriane taunted her.

"Are not!" Kara yelled.

"Am, too!" Adriane retorted.

"Not!"

"Too!"

"You think all this magic is going to make you a star?" Kara waved her arm around the room.

"Hey, you started it," Adriane said, cruel glimmers of dark delight dancing in her eyes. "You're the one who cheated. You stole the horn."

Kara's face flushed. How had Adriane discovered that?

"So don't lecture me about magic, cheater!" Adriane snickered.

Kara shook her head. "This can't be happening."

"But it is," Adriane said, walking to the table and taking a swig from a water bottle. She chucked the plastic bottle against the wall and swung her guitar into position. "You know what you are? You're a blazing *dud!* I'm the one who's going to shine tonight!"

"That's my spot and no one's going to take it from me!" Kara said angrily.

Adriane spun around and played a fast series of notes, fingers running up the guitar neck, sending out sounds so loud Kara thought they'd make her head explode. Adriane played faster and jumped, doing a split in the air. She landed, stomping her boots on the floor. A fiery crimson streak of energy ripped from the instrument and slammed into the wall, missing Kara by inches.

"Hey! This is my new jacket!"

Adriane strolled to the table and tasted a piece of cake while Kara struggled to her feet.

"I don't know what's gotten into you," Kara said quickly, "but there's only one spot open in the show. And that spot is for me!"

Adriane giggled. She gripped her guitar again. "Really? You think you're gonna be up for that, Miss Clueless, or should I say, Miss Jewel-less?"

Kara saw Adriane's lips begin to move, and a soft song rose into the air. Was Adriane *spellsinging?* Then, whirling, Adriane jammed on her guitar, letting loose another volley of crimson bolts at Kara.

But this time, Kara was ready for her. She leaped out of the way, holding up the unicorn horn like a light saber.

Desperately, she tried to remember the spellsongs she had seen. The "Spell of Silence" came to her—but the words were all scrambled. For some reason, she just couldn't remember it right. Other spellsongs flashed in her mind. All she needed was a chance, a few seconds to deliver one of the songs—

"Look at you!" Adriane sneered. "You're magically impaired!"

Kara gripped the horn tight. "Be . . . *quiet!*"

Power rippled through Kara, and Adriane darted back, her fingers moving over the frets in a blur. A crackling red shield appeared around her. The shield buckled in a half dozen places as the magic from the unicorn horn crashed into it—but it didn't yield.

"What's the problem, Kara?" Adriane asked, her guitar wailing again, crimson sparkles of energy surrounding her. "Can't take the heat? You gonna wimp out onstage, too?"

"Stop it!" Kara commanded. The table rattled with energy. A chocolate layer cake lifted and smashed into Adriane's face, making her gasp in surprise.

Kara laughed.

Wiping off the chocolate, Adriane walked to the table and eyed the row of pastries. "Messy, huh?"

Kara's eyes went wide. "Oh no! Don't even think it!"

Adriane strummed the guitar again. Kara dove into

the corner, waving the horn about, expertly defending her clothes from flying fruit, cookies, pretzels, and dip.

Kara stood up triumphantly. Then she looked down. There was a big stain right on the front pocket of her jacket! "That's it!" she screamed.

Holding up the horn, Kara sent a blazing arc of blue fire hurtling across the room, exploding into the table, sending food, dishes, and Adriane flying. Adriane landed with a graceless *oomf!* as her crimson shield faded away.

"The truth is, you don't have what it takes," Adriane shot back, rising on wobbly legs. "*I'm* the one Johnny really wants to sing with."

"You are, like, *so* deluded!" Kara said, raising the horn again. "I'm glad I took the horn!" She tingled with delight—and felt matching warmth against her heart from Johnny's locket—as Adriane's face went pale.

"So I can teach you a lesson," Kara said, advancing on the other girl. "Lesson one: You have no . . . taste!"

Kara waved the horn in a circle like a wand, releasing sparkles of magic. The posters glowed with light, and suddenly the pictures of Adriane were all replaced by images of Kara. She was dressed in the coolest outfits, singing and dancing like a star. A blazing star!

Kara smiled in satisfaction. She was ready to rock!

15

*C*AROLYN FLETCHER DROVE the green Explorer through the gates of Ravenswood. Emily sat in the passenger seat, nervously looking out the window. Cars were parked along the driveway backing up past the gate and all the way down Tioga Road. Crowds of people were walking toward the back of the preserve, some carrying picnic baskets.

"Look at all these cars," Carolyn commented. "This is really incredible, Em. And all the people! I can't wait to see Mrs. Windor's face when she—"

"*Healer!*"

Emily jumped against the shoulder strap. "Storm?"

"It's a beautiful day, hon," Carolyn said to her. "No chance of a storm."

"Come quickly!"

"What is it?" Emily frantically scanned the grounds.

"It's just a bit of traffic. Emily, are you all right?"

"Adriane has been hurt! We're at the cottage."

"Mom! Stop the car!"

"What?"

"Let me out! I have to . . . fix something!"

Carolyn pulled the car to the side as Emily bolted out the door. "I'll catch up to you later!" she yelled as she ran across the front lawn to the far side of the manor.

Storm practically bowled her over as she rounded the cobblestone path to Adriane's cottage. The mistwolf's fur bristled with distress.

"Something's happened to her," Stormbringer said.

Emily burst through the front door. Adriane was on the floor. Gran lay on the couch. Emily ran to Adriane and checked her pulse. Then she moved to check Gran.

"Ahhhh!"

Emily swung around at the scream. Ozzie stood in the doorway, mouth open. He was flanked by Lyra, Ronif, and a few other quiffles. Four pegasii stood behind him along with brimbees, wommels, and pooxim, all peering into the cottage.

Ozzie ran over and looked into Adriane's face. "She's dead!"

"No, Ozzie," Emily said calmly. "She's sleeping. So is Gran."

Ozzie flopped to the floor. "Thank goodness."

"Adriane. Adriane, wake up!" Emily called. "Storm, what happened?"

"*I felt her distress, her fear . . . then nothing.*"

"Come on, Adriane, rise and shine!" Ozzie patted the side of Adriane's face.

But no matter how hard they tried, they couldn't bring Adriane around. Gran was in the exact same state.

"Something is not right here," Emily said. She turned to all the animals that had gathered outside of the cottage.

"Everyone! Inside! Quickly!" Emily commanded. "You're supposed to be in the glade!"

The animals barreled into the cottage. Although it wasn't a small house, it was soon overstuffed with fur, beaks, flippers, and wings.

"Gather round me," Emily said.

"*Gah!* That shouldn't be hard!" Ozzie's muffled voice said.

Emily looked around for Ozzie and found him stuck between a wommel and a hard place.

Pulling him free, she settled next to Adriane and held out her wrist. Ozzie stood close as the rainbow jewel pulsed with blue-green light. Emily concentrated and sent out her healing magic to her sleeping friend. She sensed no physical injury, just a deep blackness. Adriane stirred but did not awaken

"She's in some kind of deep trance," Ozzie realized.

"A spell," Ronif said.

"Yes . . . a spell," Emily mused. "Everyone concentrate with me. Send healing strength to break the sleeping spell."

She focused her jewel and reached out again.

The wolf stone on Adriane's wrist flashed with light. Emily quickly placed her gem next to the wolf stone, willing the healing magic to flow into Adriane. Both gems flared with magic and Adriane's eyes fluttered opened. "Hey," she said groggily "Is that a ferret in my face?"

The Skultum had no idea what was happening. Not at first. He was wearing Adriane's form and had Kara fighting to give it all up onstage, just as he had planned. Then, he'd suddenly started to feel weak. His entire body trembled, his flesh crawled, and it was hard to keep posing as Adriane.

He was beginning to change. That meant his victim had awakened, which should have been impossible! The only way that spell could be broken was with . . . magic.

The other mages would know what was going on—and so would the real Adriane!

Hissing, the Skultum threw down the guitar and stumbled back, his stolen "Adriane" form losing its shape as he looked around for a way out.

Kara gasped. Adriane's face was *changing* . . . no, not

just her face, it was the girl's entire form! For a shocking, mind-splintering instant, Kara saw—or *thought* she saw—Adriane morph into Johnny and *become* the singer. His hands danced, fingers moving in complex patterns as a strange song left his lips. Then, in a heartbeat, the figure before her shimmered and transformed into a monstrous creature covered in green scales. Slivered reptile eyes shone from its hideous face. Then it was gone.

"What . . . what just happened?" Kara began, attempting to wrap her thoughts around the horrific thing she had just seen . . . or *thought* she had just seen . . .

"*Ouch!*" Johnny's locket flared red hot against her skin. She flinched and looked away. Her thoughts grew hazy, her head throbbed. Then the locket cooled and Kara felt a deep sense of triumph and exhilaration. So what if Adriane had gotten away? Kara had proved to Adriane that she was the blazing star, and now she would prove it to the world! Nothing would stand in the way of her singing the big number with Johnny! She *was* a star, baby!

Suddenly, something flew by Kara, flapping down the corridor where Adriane had disappeared. *Ewww!* A bat! A few seconds later, she heard footsteps behind her. She turned to see Johnny entering the ballroom from the entrance across the room.

The singer quickly covered the distance separating them. Concern tinged his words. "Kara, what happened? Are you all right?"

"You were right, Johnny," she told him. "Adriane wanted to sing in the spotlight. She wanted to take my place!"

"Well, don't worry. No one can take your place! I'll make sure Adriane doesn't get anywhere near you during the show."

"Thanks," Kara said, still feeling a little shaky.

Johnny smiled as he led Kara to the back door of the manor and onto the great lawn. The crowd was chanting for Johnny. His band had taken their places onstage, ready to rock.

"It's show time." Johnny straightened his leather jacket as he led Kara to the side of the stage. People covered the entire field.

"Johnny! Johnny! "

"Are you ready?" he asked Kara.

"Kara! Kara!" Did she hear the crowd shouting her name also?

"Yeah!" Kara wiped the dried stain from her jacket. "I'm ready to shine my light!"

"All right! Let's knock 'em dead!"

ADRIANE PACED BACK and forth as Emily entered the living room. "Gran's fine now. Just resting," she reported.

"We were right," Adriane said, her hands balled into fists, wolf stone pulsing.

"It's Johnny! Only it's worse than we thought . . . whatever he is, he's not human."

"A shape-shifter," Balthazar said.

"That's what we sensed the other night." Ronif shuddered.

"What're we talking about here, banshee? Sylph? Brag? Dryad?" Ozzie asked.

"Worse," Rommel answered.

"Werebeast?"

"Keep going," a pooxim sang out.

"A fairy creature then." Ozzie paced, paws behind his back.

The animals followed him, nodding in agreement.

"I thought fairies were good," Emily queried.

"Not the dark ones," Eddie the brimbee said.

The pooxim agreed. "Dark fairy creatures are extremely dangerous."

Ozzie turned to the girls. "This one is very cunning and proficient with spells." The ferret waved his paws around.

Adriane flashed on the Fairimental's warning. "Like spellsinging."

"Skultum!" Several animals said at once, their voices quivering.

"Blingo," Balthazar said. "This fairy creature is rare and very, very evil."

"*A Skultum. That explains it. It must have disguised itself as me.*" Lyra was wildly pacing now. "*I thought she was ignoring me, but maybe she can't hear me. Kara is in terrible danger! We have to help her!*"

"Skultum! " The animals all wailed. "We're no match for that magic!"

"Everyone, chill! You have to get back to the glade!" Emily said. "All of you!"

From outside, they heard the sounds of rockin' drums, a thumping bass, and a wild electric guitar.

"The show's started!" Ozzie yelled.

Then the most powerful spellsinging voice in this world—and any other—rang out. Johnny Conrad had taken the stage.

16

*D*ANCE! DANCE! DANCE! *Take a chance and dance!*

Buzzing with excitement, Kara watched from the wings as Johnny launched into his opening number. The audience loved it: moving, clapping, and dancing to the music. Johnny had them in the palm of his hand.

In her hand, Kara clutched the locket, thinking back to how she had first pictured the event, months ago. And now it was really happening! Here she was with Johnny Conrad, about to become the star she was meant to be!

She would use the magic. She had no choice. Her song with Johnny had to go perfectly.

"Kara! Kara!"

Was the crowd calling out her name already? She

scanned the rows of faces. They were all intently watching Johnny, center stage.

"Over here!"

Just outside the roped-off area beside the stage, Emily and Adriane were jumping and waving. Adriane was in her black jeans and dark green jacket. When did she have time to change? Kara wondered.

They were yelling something but she couldn't make it out above the music. Emily was arguing with the security people but the guards weren't letting them through. Kara smirked as Adriane paced back and forth, hands balled into fists. She must be so mad! Kara smiled to herself. Serves her right.

She turned back to the stage as Johnny finished his first song.

"Hello, Stonehill!" The pop star shouted. "It's a great night for Ravenswood!"

The audience exploded in applause. Then the band blazed into their second number. Johnny rocked out, doing the moves that had made him famous.

Kara danced in the wings, jumping and—*ow!* Something had just bitten her! She spun around but nothing was there. Another spark stung her leg. What was that? Then she caught a telltale flash of amber light. *Zing!* She'd been bitten again! Adriane! Angry, she whirled around and saw the black-haired girl standing, arm raised, golden light flaring from her jewel. Kara narrowed her eyes and stuck her tongue out. She was just starting to turn away when she saw Adriane pointing. Kara followed Adriane's finger. Emily was holding up a sign. IT WASN'T LYRA!

Kara stopped moving. It wasn't Lyra? She loved Lyra more than anyone, but she'd been avoiding the cat. In fact, she hadn't even really thought of her since . . . *it wasn't Lyra!*

Something twisted in her stomach. She looked back at Emily again, who now had a second sign raised. IT WASN'T ADRIANE!

What did Emily mean? Lyra and Adriane had been *horrible* to her. Of course it was them! She'd seen them! A tingle of fear crept up Kara's back, tickling its way to her neck. She took a tentative step toward her friends.

Suddenly, the locket around her neck sparked with intense heat. Her mind became hazy. Johnny was finishing his second number, but he was looking directly at her, anger flaring across his face. Kara shook her head—she must be crazy! She turned back to the stage and was relieved to see Johnny's look soften before he faced the crowd and bowed.

"Before we continue," he announced. "I know you're all excited about the contest. And I have picked the winner!"

What? Kara's face mirrored the surprise on the contestants'—no one had performed yet!

Johnny continued, "Let's hear it for the person who made this whole day possible, Ravenswood's very own, Kara Davies!"

Applause thundered as Johnny beckoned Kara. In a daze, she stepped onstage.

"And we have a surprise for you—we're going to perform a brand-new song dedicated to the Ravenswood Preserve!" Johnny smiled at Kara. "Give it all you got!"

He nodded to the band, and the music started. Kara felt light-headed.

The audience sat waiting as the band reached her cue. Kara opened her mouth and sang.

In a world that spins so fast
Nothing real seems to last
When the future falls out of sight
Find the path and shine your light

Kara scanned the crowd and felt her cheeks flush. Wincing, she spied Heather flanked by Molly and Tiffany, all snickering. This was awful. Kara's voice hadn't changed a bit.

"Sing it! Johnny hissed. "You're the star! Make it happen! Use your star power."

The locket around her neck flared with magical energy. Kara thought, when they see what kind of star I really am, they'll come back to me.

She *deserved* to be the blazing star. That was her destiny, and Johnny could make it happen.

Reaching into her jacket, she felt the comforting coolness

of the unicorn horn. Gripping it tightly, she called upon its magic . . . and sang.

Kara's voice suddenly soared into the air, hitting perfect notes. She sang louder, moving her feet to the backbeat.

Johnny jumped into the air and danced. "That's it!"

The audience cheered.

As Kara sang the chorus, she could feel the powerful energies flowing from the unicorn horn mixing it up with her magic. Lights behind the stage flashed in time to the beat as a wave of blue light pulsed around her.

Johnny was ecstatic. "Beautiful! More! Give it more! Shine your light!"

And she did.

17

I N THE DISTANCE, away from the surging crowd, strong magic swirled into the large field. The portal to Ravenswood opened wide, ripping the air with shrieking winds against the darkening horizon. The sparkling dreamcatcher that kept Ravenswood safe stretched across it, ready to amplify any magic sent into it.

EMILY AND ADRIANE were pushed to the side of the great lawn as people surged forward to get closer to the stage. "*Warrior! Healer!*" The girls heard the mistwolf's urgent voice in their heads.

"What is it, Storm?" Adriane asked.

"*The portal has opened!*"

"Oh, no!"

The girls looked back up at Kara and saw the blue glow around her. That wasn't special effects! That was magic!

They pushed and shoved their way to the stage.

"Kara, stop!" Emily called. "You're opening the portal!"

Kara heard them and faltered. But before she could react, there was a blast of magic from the locket—and suddenly she was singing louder than ever, releasing more and more of her magic.

"Johnny!" Adriane shouted, nodding toward the wildly grinning singer. "He's making her do it!"

And though Kara was singing wonderfully, there was pain and fear in her eyes.

The bass thrummed a thumping rhythm, and the band began its instrumental break. Johnny pumped his fist in the air as he swaggered across the stage, drawing the crowd to their feet.

His fingers reached into the sky and he began to spin. A blistering lead solo kept the fevered pace. Suddenly the music stopped—and so did Johnny. In his hands he cradled a ball of light.

He grinned at the audience as the ball grew brighter, revealing twinkling stars inside. The crowd cheered louder.

With a graceful toss, he sent the ball floating gently over his head. It sparkled as it caught the stage lights, glistening like a mirror ball, sailing through the air right toward Kara.

Kara recognized it instantly, the twinkling ball of stars with the bright silver glow in its center. She was looking at the fairy map. The gift the Fairimentals had given her. The one stolen last summer by the monstrous manticore.

Kara gazed at Johnny in fear. Then she felt the heat of the locket on her skin, pulling at her magic, and her thoughts began to get hazy. In a burst of sudden panic, she tightened her grip on the unicorn horn.

"What have I done," Kara said, her voice breaking as the tears welled in her eyes, blurring her vision.

But Johnny was no longer looking at her. His gaze was firmly fixed on the fairy map.

"You are the blazing star." His musical voice sounded like a chant. "Shine on!"

The fairy map began to settle around her, covering her in dazzling stars. Pinpoints of light twinkled, each a portal on the magic web.

"Sing, Kara!" Johnny urged. "Make it happen."

The audience was on its feet, breathlessly waiting to see what would follow this special effects extravaganza.

Kara struggled to fight Johnny's spell and stop the song before it was too late, but she didn't have the strength. The unicorn horn could not protect her. Triggered by her blazing star power, the lights in the fairy map rolled and tumbled, falling into a pattern.

And she was just another falling star about to flame out in a blaze of glory.

No! She *had* to fight this! "Lyra!" she called out.

"*I'm here!*" the cat answered.

Hearing the voice of her best friend, Kara suddenly knew that Lyra would never do anything to hurt her. It had all been a trick.

Kara started the next verse—but reaching out to her friend for strength, she changed the words.

A web of lies spins so fast
I was blinded by your night
We can see the truth at last
Let's all shine our light!

The crowd gasped. Her voice sounded horrible. She couldn't hit any of the notes.

"What's she doing?" Emily asked nervously.

"She's changing the words," Adriane said, surprised. "She's trying to spellsing!"

Suddenly, a chill wind kicked up and surrounded Johnny. In fury, he swung around and glared at Kara. What was that girl doing? Opening his mouth, he joined her in song, tightening his control, forcing Kara to sing the right words to his spell.

Kara tried to sing again, but she could barely catch her breath.

Emily and Adriane raced to the stage. Security guards converged on them.

"You have to let us through!" Adriane demanded.

"We told you, no one's allowed on stage during the show!"

"Perhaps you'd like to talk to the ones that run this place." Emily stepped aside to reveal Stormbringer and Lyra.

The animals bared their teeth and growled fiercely.

"Whoa!" The guard jumped back at the sight of the huge silver wolf and the large spotted cat. "No problem!"

Adriane pulled the animals back. "Thanks, guys. We'll take it from here."

Her gaze fell on the locket around Kara's neck, glowing with dark magic.

"*That's* what Johnny's using to control Kara!" Without a second thought, Adriane launched herself on stage. She ran to Kara and knocked the fairy map away from her. The ball floated gently over the crowd.

People in the audience started to bat it around like a translucent beach ball.

Rage flared on Johnny's face, but only for a second. Dancing to the edge of the stage, he motioned for the crowd to send the ball back to him.

Adriane surged toward Kara, her hand reaching for the locket—but she was yanked back. Another burly guard carried the struggling girl back to the wings.

A sudden awareness flooded into Kara. The fairy map was always meant for her. That's what Johnny really wanted. Only she could open it—and find Avalon.

She heard Johnny. "Kara, you are the blazing star—now *finish* the spell!"

Wide-eyed with horror, Kara realized the terrible mistake she'd made—all the wrong decisions and all the wrong excuses to justify them.

She felt herself spiraling out of control. The locket that seemed to complete her, focus, and sharpen her magic, was a lie. Just like the dark magic Johnny had worked on her.

She had to sing.

It was her dream.

Her *nightmare.*

There was a loud commotion backstage. Kara heard growls, scuffling, and people running. Then Adriane was racing toward her, reaching for the locket. Kara had a flash that this was a mistake, the worst mistake anyone could make.

Or maybe that was just what Johnny wanted her to think.

Adriane's hand closed over the locket—

And for a single instant, Kara and Adriane's minds were linked. Kara understood that Adriane hadn't grabbed the locket for the sake of Ravenswood, or for Avalon, or even to protect herself; her only thought was to help her friend. Kara had been so wrong.

The chain securing the locket snapped—and Adriane threw it down, crushing it with her boot. Kara looked at Adriane, her eyes brimming with tears.

Adriane just nodded.

Howling with rage, Johnny ran around the stage, gesturing and singing wildly.

The fairy map floated above the audience as they bounced it to and fro. Bright stars moved inside it in shifting patterns.

If anyone had been in the open field just behind the trees, they might have seen a much larger light show. Paths of stars swirled in the portal as the blazing star's magic created a chain reaction. Other portals opened one by one in a frantic tumbling of cosmic dominoes.

Johnny sang and a swirling cloud of intense energy formed several feet above his head. Deep shades of red and blue blended together as bolts of lightening shot out from its center, reaching for the fairy map. Suddenly, something else bobbed up into the air above the audience. It swatted the fairy map away then fell back into the crowd.

"What is that?" Emily asked.

Some sort of furry animal was being tossed into the air above the heads of the crowd.

"Ozzie!" Emily cried.

"Woot!" the ferret chortled as the crowd flipped him head over paws. Each time Ozzie flew into the air he swiped at the fairy map, knocking it away from Johnny's grasp.

But all eyes were fixed on Kara, who was shining in a diamond-white light that bathed the stage and the crowd.

Kara tried desperately to control her magic, but it was too late. She had changed, and not in the way she had imagined. She had betrayed her friends and the bright light inside had turned—to darkness.

Suddenly, a loud guitar chord rang out over the crowd. An enormous cheer rose up.

Adriane was standing beside Kara, guitar in hand. "Let's rock and roll!"

Grasping her friend's magic, Kara wrapped herself in the warrior's strength. Together they sang, their voices mixing in magical harmony.

Together we stand strong
Together we can make it right
When everything feels wrong
Let's shine our light!

Clouds of white crystals rose from Kara, filling the air with beautiful sounds and washing away Johnny's swirling pattern.

Whirling around to signal his band, Johnny switched to another tune, his voice thundering out over the stage.

Tossing his head back, he howled a spellsong that mor-phed the mages' magic. A roaring phoenix of red fire rose into the sky, opening its maw as if to bake the girls where they stood.

Kara held the unicorn horn tight and magic leaped forth. A blue-white unicorn formed in the air. The sparkling image reared back and charged the phoenix, impaling the fire creature with its horn. Cool silver sparkles rained down on the amazed audience as the images vanished.

Johnny launched into a smoldering version of the title song from his new CD.

I put a spell on you,
One look in my eyes, you know it's true
One note of my voice tells you what to do
Don't you know, I put a spell on you

Adriane's guitar squealed in feedback and sparks flew. The girls' voices faded as they began to sway under the spell of the song.

Suddenly, the sound of a flute sent an achingly beau-tiful melody arcing over the crowd. It was Emily. She stood next to Kara and Adriane. Playing her flute, she sent out the song of Lorelei, the song of friendship she shared with the unicorn.

Johnny stopped singing. Was he weakening?

"Come on, girls," Kara yelled. "Let's kick it!"

One chance for us all to stand together
One hope it's going to last forever
We've got the spirit
We're going to make it
I know the magic's on our side

Kara's voice sounded like . . . Kara's voice, but to her friends it was the voice of an angel.

"Everybody help us! Join in!" Kara called out.

The entire audience sang with the girls.

Johnny was quivering, shimmering in lights. Be*Tween's song carried powerful magic. He ran behind the amplifiers as his human form began to melt away, twisting into a green, scaly monster.

Kara saw a dark shadow and caught sight of a bat flying away from the stage. She stood between Adriane and Emily and held out her hands. Adriane and Emily clasped hands with their friend, raising their arms high. A bolt of magic flew from the mages, arcing out into the evening sky.

Fireworks lit up the night as the Skultum was swept into the dreamcatcher and pulled into the swirling vortex. The portal closed.

For several long moments there was nothing but silence on the great lawn of Ravenswood. Then someone in the audience started clapping and others joined in. The audience surged to its feet, crying out for more!

Kara embraced her friends as they took a bow to a

thundering round of applause. The band was looking around uncertainly for Johnny.

Holding the mike, Kara announced, "Johnny had to fly. But, before we go, I'd like to invite all the contestants to sing with us. Tonight, we're all stars!"

The excited girls and guys rushed onstage, surrounding Kara, Emily, and Adriane.

"I'd like our special animal friends to join us, too. They are the spirit of Ravenswood. Let's have a big hand for Stormbringer!"

The crowd cheered as the silver wolf loped on stage and stood next to Adriane.

"My best friend ever, Lyra!"

Lyra padded over to Kara. Kara knelt and hugged the cat so tightly, Lyra thought she would burst.

"Ariel!" Emily shouted out.

The snowy owl swooped over the astonished crowd and landed on Emily's arm.

Adriane took the mike. "And the one and only rock and roll ferret, Ozzie!"

The crowd went crazy cheering as Ozzie scampered onstage, pumping his paws in the air.

Kara turned to Heather and smiled. "You start."

Heather smiled back and sang.

We've got the spirit
We're going to make it
I know the magic's on our side

We've got the power in the darkest hour
So don't give up the Spirit of Avalon

Everyone sang together. Their voices joined as one and they sang from their hearts, sending the sweetest, truest, most powerful magic ringing out across the preserve, across their world, and across the magic web to what lay beyond.

18

"*I*'VE NEVER SEEN so many messages," Ozzie called out. The ferret was at the library computer reading through the hundreds of e-mails that had been pouring in from all over the world.

Congrats on a great show!
The special effects were awesome!
Are you available to appear in Springfield?
Ravenswood rules!

"We haven't finished the 'I told you so's' yet." Adriane paced the floor of the library, throwing her arms in the air. "You and magic, Kara! It's like throwing gasoline on fire!"

Kara nodded, eyes lowered. Emily was there, too, along with Storm, Lyra, Ronif, Rasha, and Balthazar. The unicorn horn lay on the table where Kara had put it—after she had confessed everything. Next to the crystal horn, the glowing orb of stars twinkled, tiny points of light inside configured in a still unknown pattern.

It had taken most of Sunday to get the great lawn cleaned up. It would still take some weeks before everything was back to normal. If that would *ever* be possible.

But all Kara thought about was how much she'd wanted to believe Johnny's lies, how her selfish emotions had triggered her magic in all the wrong ways. She had really messed up big time. Why couldn't she make good magic like the others? Even after all this time, she had no better control over the magic than when she had first discovered it—maybe even worse. She was supposed to be part of a team, building trust and confidence, not destroying everything they worked so hard for—like the friendships she had almost so carelessly thrown away.

She leaned into Lyra, hugging her friend quietly.

"Ha! Check this out," the ferret said. "Teen singer, Johnny Conrad, rejoined his band for a show in Memphis. When asked about the successful benefit performance at Ravenswood, he seemed in a daze and couldn't remember the show!"

Emily looked over the ferret's shoulder. "Well, at least he's okay."

"Great!" Kara was on her feet. "The *real* Johnny Conrad won't remember anything!" she exclaimed. Kara's star had come and gone.

"Here's one from the Town Council," Ozzie said.

Congratulations on a terrific event. Stonehill has been on the news all day. The Ravenswood Wildlife Preserve and Ravenswood Manor have been marked for landmark status. We need someone to represent the town, any suggestions?

Adriane ran to the screen. "Wow. That's incredible!"

"How bout that, Kara?" Emily said.

Kara hopped to her feet. "Tell them to send Mrs. Windor," she said, walking to the window.

The others stared at her.

"Let *her* take the credit. I've had my time in the spot-light," she said wistfully.

Emily glanced at Adriane and nudged her. "You were also under the creature's spell, Adriane."

"Yeah," Adriane sighed. "And I'm really sorry about the way I acted. Really sorry, Kara."

"I know." Kara half smiled. "Thanks. But you broke your spell. I couldn't."

"Because of this." Adriane held up her wrist. Her wolf

stone sparkled with amber light. A stern look from Emily made the warrior quickly cover her jewel.

"It's okay, you can say it. We all know I don't have a jewel."

"And that's why Johnny—whatever it was—was able to control you for so long," Emily said. "That locket acted like a magic jewel, focusing your magic."

"Only it wasn't *good* magic," Kara stated. "Just like the last jewel I didn't have."

Emily continued gently, "And when you find your jewel, it will be totally amazing—"

"I'll *never* find one!" Kara burst out.

"We don't know that, Kara."

Kara turned away as the others waited.

"We got the fairy map back," Ronif offered. "That's a major victory."

"But I don't even know what I did!" Kara cried, glancing at the glowing orb. "Did I open the path to Avalon or not? The Dark Sorceress could be there right now!"

She stared sadly out the window. "I should have known what the Fairimentals were trying to say to me."

"What's that?" Adriane asked.

"They said, 'Spellsing as three.' Not one, but three."

"And that's what we did," Emily said. "We beat that monster by singing together, as three."

"Both of you have done so much. All I do is ruin everything I touch."

"*That's not true, Kara,*" Lyra brushed against her. "*You helped me grow back my fur.*"

"That was a mistake," Kara started. "I didn't mean . . . oh, I didn't know what I was doing!"

"We're all learning as we go, Kara," Ozzie said. "We're bound to make mistakes."

"Not like this one. And what about the next time? Am I going to turn against my friends when they need me? Or worse?" She hung her head, letting her long blond hair fall over her face.

"Kara, what are you saying?" Adriane asked.

"I . . . I'm just not good at magic and I hate being not good at anything! I'm not going to use magic any more. I'll help out with the Town Council, but you're going to have to find another mage."

"Kara, you're our friend," Emily pleaded. "You can't leave."

"Emily, that's exactly why I have to." Kara faced the other girls and animals. "You guys *are* my friends . . . and I can't keep getting you in trouble. I just want to go back to being normal."

"Priority e-mail!" Ozzie called out.

The girls looked over the ferret's head at a bright icon arcing across the browser. It looked like a small shooting star.

"What kind of icon is that?" Adriane asked

Ozzie clicked on the star. It was a file folder containing a message.

Your concert was wonderful. We're sorry we could
not be there. Stand ready, mages. The portals have
opened and now your trials have just begun. You
must go forward, together as three, and alone as a
healer, a warrior, and a blazing star. It is time to follow your path . . . and come home.
The magic is with you, now and forever.
Be*Tween

"Be*Tween!" Kara said, amazed. "They know about
the magic?"

"It seems our journey is about to take a turn," Emily
said.

"Do we go forward as three?" Adriane asked.

"Four, actually," Ozzie corrected her.

Emily, Adriane, and the others turned to Kara, waiting for her to make her decision.

Whatever she chose to do, Adriane, Emily, and Ozzie
would have to deal with the situation whether they liked
it or not. Maybe Kara just wasn't cut out to be the blazing star. They would just have to wait and see.

Epilogue

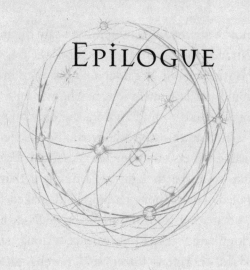

*T*HE DARK SORCERESS stood in her lair, hidden
beneath the sands of the burned out desert. With a
claw-tipped finger, she swirled the waters of her scrying
pool and the images appeared. The ruined land known as
the Shadowlands—once one of the most beautiful forests
in Aldenmor—fluttered in the crimson waters.
Blackened husks and dust littered the ground where towering trees had grown only a few short years ago.

Sacrifices must be made, she thought. Magical energies swept through her long, silver hair as she raised her
arms. With a sweep of her hands the image shifted,
zooming out above the desert dunes where golden hues
of the sky peeked through the dark cloud layer of Black

Fire. The image zoomed further until she saw the magic web itself, strands torn and frayed, old and weak.

Time was running out. Without an infusion of magic, the web would not last much longer. She was in a race with the Fairimentals to find Avalon, the only hope for saving the web. And this time, she would be the victor.

The swirling waters shimmered and settled. Peering into the inky void, she thought for a moment that her spell had failed. Then a bone chilling cold snaked from the image, emanating from the towering walls of black ice that dominated the Otherworlds. Along sheer, gleaming slabs, enormous frozen spider webs glittered with silent menace.

The echo of footsteps skittered across the polished floor. The sorceress recoiled as a misshapen shadow stretched across the ice. Eight legs moved beneath a wide robe. Faceted yellow insect eyes blinked coldly within a dark cowl. The one she sought was there, waiting for her.

Unlike the wretched Skultum, this being, that used to be her friend, could not change her form at a moment's urging . . . though what she saw was so repulsive, she almost wished that it could.

"Well, well, Miranda. I thought you'd forgotten your old friends," the Spider Witch's voice grated with a cold, inhuman clicking.

The sorceress sneered. "It's time."

She didn't look at the creature directly. The sight of it disgusted her, perhaps because the same fate could easily have befallen her—and still might if she was not careful. But the Spider Witch's transformation had given her incredible power, and the sorceress needed her old friend—for now.

"You plan to open the Gates of Avalon again?" The Spider Witch clicked hard mandibles beneath her cowl. The sorceress realized the creature was laughing at her. "You have no key, remember?"

How could she forget? Building the key to Avalon had been her life's work until—

"I have a plan. I will draw the magic I need into my crystals and make another key. Once I open the gates, I will use the magic of Avalon to open the Otherworlds. You will then be free to reweave the web."

"A web woven with the magic of Avalon," the Spider Witch clicked, relishing the idea.

"One we control."

Antennae flicked beneath the witch's cowl. "You were the one that got me locked in here in the first place. How do I know I can trust you?"

"The Fairimentals trapped you in the Otherworlds, not I!"

"Nonetheless . . ." The Spider Witch moved slowly, her legs clicking on the black ice. "What makes this time different? The Fairimentals have proven their ability to be . . . shall we say, lucky."

"I have the fairy map that holds the path to Avalon."

The sound of flickering wings buzzed from the Spider

Witch. "And who shall open this fairy map? The blazing star is dead and I am reasonably sure the map was not given to you."

The sorceress calmed herself. "Three new mages have been chosen to stand for the Fairimentals . . . including a young blazing star."

"Interesting." The witch stopped pacing. "Go on."

"They are unschooled in magic. Only one is powerful enough to do what is required. The map was given to her. She does not possess a jewel so her magic is wild, untamed, and driven by emotion."

"What makes you so sure this blazing star can open the map?"

"She already has." A wicked smile crossed her red lips as the sorceress flicked a strand of lightning slashed hair from her face.

Several long minutes passed before the Spider Witch spoke again.

"Three mages, you say."

"The blazing star, a warrior . . . and a healer."

"A healer? Oh, now this is very interesting. Can she weave magic as well?"

"Of course not. These mages have no mentor."

"Was not Gardener supposed to train the new mages?"

"That old wizard will be no threat to us."

The Spider Witch skittered forward and the Dark Sorceress gasped. It seemed close enough to touch her.

"If your plan succeeds, I will reweave the web and control half. Be content I do not take more."

The Dark Sorceress trembled in anger, but held herself in check.

"I look forward to returning to my lair. Just like old times." The Spider Witch bowed as the image swirled and faded away.

A bitter breeze caressed the pale flesh of the Dark Sorceress's strained face. She grasped the stone pedestal as the magic sickness wracked her body. This had been a bold move, using so much of her precious magic. But the time had come for bold moves. She knew her old friend could not resist going after the magic of Avalon again—even if it was the same dark magic that had transformed her into a hideous creature. Her arrogance still made the sorceress rage inside.

Patience, she told herself, closing her eyes. At Mt. Hope, the Skultum was fast approaching his goal. The mistwolves would fall. Their magic would bring the Dark Sorceress one step closer toward securing her future . . . and her eternal existence.

Bestiary &
Creature Guide

Skultum

AFFILIATION: EVIL

*T*he Skultum is a dark fairy creature. A master of tricks and illusions, the Skultum is a shapeshifter with potent transformational powers. It uses spellsinging to lull victims into a sleep state so it can replicate the victim's form. Being fairy in nature, if you can get a Skultum to reveal its true name, you can absorb all its powers.

Earth Fairimental

AFFILIATION: Good

*O*ne of the four elemental guardians of Aldenmor, the Earth Fairimental is made of magic rooted deep in the elements of earth. It takes form using bits of rocks, twigs, and trees. Like all Fairimentals, the Earth Fairimental's magic is tied to Aldenmor and can only appear on Earth for very short periods of time

ARIEL, OWL
AFFILIATION: Good

*A*riel was the first creature Emily healed by herself and has a special bond with the healer. A snow owl with white feathers and wingtips of turquoise, lavender, and gold, Ariel is a very loyal and loving companion and a key member of Avalon's Team Magic. Ariel communicates telepathically but her verbal skills are improving all the time.

Brimbee

Affiliation: Good

*R*esembling large blue rabbits with iridescent purple spots, brimbees are fun loving, magically imbued animals that inhabit just about every region on Aldenmor. Brimbees have a definite mind of their own and can be boisterous and outspoken. They are not very far up the magic chain, but put a pack of brimbees together and look out!

Rachel Roberts on the Magic of Music

*P*laying in the school band and singing along to my favorite songs with my friends are some of the greatest memories I have. Music plays a key part in the Avalon series because there's nothing like good music to spread good magic. That's why I've always got a song playing while I'm writing. Music is a great way to express yourself, whether you're playing an instrument or howling along with the nearest mistwolf. If it's heartfelt and sincere, it always makes magic. And you just might create a sound that's all yours and inspire someone else.